THE GOOD SHIP SPIDER QUEEN

The Good Ship Spider Queen

Written and Illustrated by

Eda and Richard Crist

THE BOBBS MERRILL-COMPANY, INC.

PUBLISHERS

INDIANAPOLIS NEW YORK

PRINTED IN THE UNITED STATES OF AMERICA
Library of Congress Catalog Card Number: 53-5243

First Edition

We dedicate this story to Mr. Ziggley—to compensate for his loss of dignity

CONTENTS

THE GOOD SHIP SPIDER QUEEN

Chapter I

Visitor from the Tropics

MARVIN TUCKER, JR., pumped his bicycle across the old wooden canal bridge, then settled in the seat for a fast coast down the rest of Pickett Street. Passing the rough brick wall of the Towpath Inn, he picked up speed. He whizzed past Mrs. Binney's antique shop and his own house, slowed a little at the town hall, bumped across River Street, and stopped in front of Pratt's Grocery Store with a jerk that threw his cap to the ground.

He parked his bike. Then he pushed back his scattered blond hair, picked up his cap and went in.

"Is that all for today, Mr. Pratt?"

The old grocer looked up from the counter, where he was figuring a bill. "No more deliveries. But I'll need some potatoes weighed up—ten-pound bags." He pursed his lips and rubbed the fuzzy gray hair on one side of his head with his pencil. "You been steamin' around all morning, like someone gave you a hot foot. Must be you don't aim to be late for your class picnic."

Marvin, thirteen, who had a keen appreciation of such things as picnics, smiled to think of the fun he would have. A softball game, or fooling around at the creek. If he hurried with the potato weighing, he probably would get there on time.

He went into the back room, tossed his cap onto a stem of green bananas, and dragged a burlap sack of potatoes to the scales. Then he drew a stool to the open window and began the dusty job of filling paper bags.

As he worked, the familiar sound of falling water outside lured his attention from the scales. Soon he was leaning out the window, his elbows resting on the sill.

Just below, Kinnecong Creek spilled over the mill-pond dam in a watery turmoil that whirled and tumbled to its near-by outlet in the Delaware River. On the opposite bank was an old stone mill, now a summer theater and a very busy place on warm summer evenings. But at this midday hour the only activity in its yard was the movement of a small group of scenery painters leisurely applying pink paint to some canvas flats for next week's show.

Marvin idly watched this bit of slow motion for a minute. It made him drowsy, and he shifted his gaze to the millpond. A small board turned slowly on its surface, moving through some arrowhead leaves toward the crest of the dam. With a sudden burst of speed it went over the edge. It shot up through the spray at the bottom, then went bobbing among the rocks and whirlpools to the calmer water of the outlet.

He leaned farther out the window to watch the slow shore current of the river take over the work of moving the board on to the ocean. It was a long way to the ocean, he thought. Too far to go in a small boat. At least, in the tub of a rowboat that he and Eddie Pennypacker were going to buy. But the rowboat, with the sail they'd put on it, would take them to closer places that would be just as much fun. Locust Island for instance. That was only two miles down the river, but it would be exciting because there'd be bugs on it. New ones for his collection. Even the name of the island promised good hunting—though Old Cappy had said it was named for its big locust trees.

"Hey, Marvin!" somebody yelled.

Marvin looked toward the River Street bridge that spanned the millpond. His friend and fellow bug-catcher, Eddie Pennypacker, was draped on the railing, squinting up at him.

"How long are you going to be?" Eddie hollered. "Some of the kids have gone already."

"Oh, not long. I'll stop at your place on the way."

Eddie walked on and Marvin dropped two potatoes in a bag. He tossed two more in after them, but his thoughts were beginning to wander again. He jumped up and went over to a shelf. Very carefully he took down a glass mayonnaise jar with holes punched in the lid. Inside, poised on eight velvet legs and staring into Marvin's freckled face, was a large banana spider.

The black visitor from Central America had arrived in the stalk of bananas delivered that morning. It had been detected by Marvin's sharp eyes. The spider had been swiftly clapped into the jar, and now she was being sullen about it.

"Gee!" whispered Marvin as he peered through the glass. "She's sure the prettiest thing *I* ever saw. She . . . she's the queen of all the spiders!"

Suddenly his smile turned into a broad grin. Tucked under the lid was a silken ball of eggs! The spider had not been too sullen to attend to important business that morning.

Marvin slipped the jar into a small paper bag, then he counted the bags of weighed potatoes.

Sticking his head through the doorway, he asked, "Are six enough, Mr. Pratt?"

"That's enough," said the grocer. He was putting packages into a cardboard carton for a customer. "Need anything else, Mrs. Van Trant? Sugar? Bluing? How about some gherkins for the boiled ham?"

"The gherkins, and *please* hurry!" Mrs. Van Trant tapped her foot. "The club ladies will arrive in an hour."

Marvin, whistling "Riders in the Dust Ki-yay," started for the front door.

"Morning, Mrs. Van Trant," he said pleasantly. He started to tip his cap but discovered he had forgotten it. He set his package on the counter and went back to the storage room. The scenery painters had finished the pink flats and were now starting on a wallboard tree. One painter was covering the trunk with dark brown and the others were smearing two shades of green over the leaves.

I could do that, thought Marvin. I'll bet I could even act in a play if they'd let me.

He slapped his cap over one eye and raised a threatening arm. "I'm givin' you fair and square warnin'!" he said gruffly. "I'm a deputy of the law, and my swore duty is t' run you range varmints clean out o' the Bar-B valley. Now head fer the pass 'fore I blast you with my six-shootin' gherkin!"

He straightened his cap and once again started out.

He searched up and down the counter for the bag that held his spider, but it wasn't there. He went around the end of the counter and looked on the floor behind it. The spider was gone!

As Mrs. Van Trant's car roared off, Mr. Pratt came into the store. "Better get some bars for the back window," he said. "The super market was robbed last night. First holdup around here for years, but there's no tellin'——" He broke off and looked questioningly at Marvin. "Lose something?"

"I've lost my . . . " Marvin began. But a horrible thought stopped him. "It's nothing, Mr. Pratt," he added hurriedly. "Just . . . just something . . . I mean nothing. I'll be back tomorrow."

He dashed out of the store and leaped onto his bike. When he rounded the corner he saw that it was no use to try to catch up with Mrs. Van Trant. Already her car was curving out of sight down River Street. Her home was too far away for him to follow her out there and get back for the school picnic. But if he didn't go and she found the spider . . . Golly, if he'd just been more careful about where he had set that bag! Sure as anything Mr. Pratt had put the spider into her carton with the other packages.

Marvin stopped his bike, then stared at his shoes. "The picnic," he said aloud, "or the spider?"

A clean decision was impossible; so he picked up a flat stone, spat on one side of it, and tossed it into the air. Stooping over the spot where it fell, he chanted, "Wet side up and dry side down, if I change my mind I hope to drown."

With his conscience thus cleared of the spider, he quickly pedaled the short distance up Pickett Street to his house. He propped his bike against the front porch and went in.

"Hey, Mom!" he called. "I'm here! Where's my picnic stuff?"

"In the refrigerator," answered his mother from upstairs.

He went into the kitchen and got his box of lunch.

Suddenly he had an inspiration. He put the lunch down, went to the telephone in the living room, looked for a number, then picked up the receiver.

"Two, five, two," he said, and waited.

"Hello. Who's callin'?" said a husky voice at the other end of the line.

"This is Marvin Tucker. Is this Mrs. Van Trant?"

"No, sir, she's not here. This is Mrs. Van Trant's maid."

"Oh. . . . Well," said Marvin, "will you please ask her to take care of the black spider?"

"What's that?"

"Black spider," repeated Marvin. "She hasn't eaten today, so a couple of flies——"

The maid's voice climbed to a higher pitch. *"Flies?* You got the right party on the phone? You want Mrs. Van Trant?"

"Yes," said Marvin impatiently. "She eats flies and

has some eggs. Just two will be plenty until I can get there. Two flies, I mean, if you will be kind enough to—"

Just then Marvin's ten-year-old brother Emery came into the house. The screen door slammed behind him.

"Kind enough to what?" he inquired, going over to Marvin.

"Wh-what did you say, mister?" asked the maid.

"Who you talking to?" Emery asked.

"—kind enough to take care of it for me," continued Marvin, ignoring Emery's remark but swinging a fast one with his foot in his direction.

Emery dodged but skidded on a braided rug. He shot across the room on one leg before losing his balance. The following crash brought down a stand on which there was a stack of plastic phonograph records. They rolled in all directions, ringing against the andirons and fireplace tools, plunking on tin wastebaskets, the furniture and the woodwork.

"Jackpot," muttered Emery from the floor.

Marvin waited until the last record made the last plink against a floor-lamp base, then he continued his phone conversation. "I'll appreciate it a lot, Miss . . . er, Madam. . . . Hello? Hello?" The line was still open, but there was no answer. In a minute or two he gave up. "Well, good-by," he said as he put the receiver down.

He got his lunch and gave Emery, who was still on the floor, his number-one scowl. It wasn't easy to keep the scowl trained on Emery and at the same time avoid stepping on records all the way to the front door. But by using the corners of his eyes, he did it.

Outside he mounted his bike, and pedaled over the canal bridge. He stopped at the second house on the other side and hollered for Eddie.

Eddie appeared with his bike. "I got a stag beetle this morning," he said importantly as they started up the street.

"Gee," said Marvin, "a live one?"

"Yep." Eddie took his cap off and put it on his picnic box, in the handle-bar basket. He had just had his blondish-red hair cut very short, and his ears seemed much too big. "Found him starting across the sidewalk up by the old cannon. Boy, you ought to see the size of his horns! Mean-looking too! Probably the biggest and meanest-looking stag beetle ever found in Shalerville."

Marvin's envy of Eddie's remarkable good fortune lasted for only a moment. "I've got something, too," he said. "I mean, I *did* have and I'll get it back."

"What?"

"The biggest doggoned spider you ever saw. And it's from tropical Central America." Marvin paused long enough to let his friend be impressed, then went on: "Mrs. Van Trant has it now."

"Mrs. Van Trant!" exclaimed Eddie, surprised. "Does *she* like spiders?"

"Don't know why she wouldn't."

Marvin explained what had happened and invited Eddie to go with him the next day to reclaim his prize.

"The Van Trants have a big lily pond in their front yard," he added. "I've always wanted to look it over, and this'll be a good chance."

"Yeah!" Eddie grinned with interest. "Water bugs . . ."

Chapter 2

The Picnic

At the edge of town Pickett Street became a black-top country road which wound through the narrow valley of Kinnecong Creek. A half mile out there was another old mill, but this one hadn't been made into something else. Its gray stone walls rose like a jungle ruin from a tangled mass of weeds, vines and age-old willows. Its great wooden wheel, sagging with age, cast mossy reflections on a dark, weed-spotted pool. Though a cascade of rubbish marred the slope at one end of the mill, it was the finest spot in the neighborhood of Shalerville for the picnic.

The members of the seventh-going-into-eighth grade

had already gathered when Marvin and Eddie arrived. Miss Phyfe, the teacher, and a dozen giggling girls were fussing with lunch baskets on the long, weathered picnic table. Several boys were taking turns at chinning themselves on a willow branch. A noisy softball game was in progress, and there was a small group of boys by the creek, poking at something in the water.

Marvin and Eddie leaned their bicycles against a tree and went over to the table with their lunches. Miss Phyfe looked up, her rosy face beaming under a wide, pink straw hat.

"Oh, hello, Marvin," she said. "And Edward—you *do* look cool in your summer haircut."

"Yes, I feel cool," Eddie said.

Marvin picked up an orange that was in the grass at his feet. "Hello, Miss Phyfe," he said. "Is this your orange?"

"Dear me, yes!" She smiled, taking the orange. "Thank you so much."

Her voice, Marvin thought, was a lot different from the one she had used all winter in the classroom. It was kind of a rested voice, and it made her seem like someone else.

"Shall we leave our lunches on the table?" Eddie asked her. "Are we going to eat soon?"

"Yes to both questions. Run along. We'll call you."

Marvin and Eddie trotted off toward the creek.

"I wonder what they're all staring at down there," Eddie said.

"Probably a crab or something," guessed Marvin. "There's a lot of them along the creek."

Just as they reached the bank, Bill Hostetter, one of the group, dragged a dripping tin box from the water and set it on a rock.

"What's that?" asked Eddie, looking over Bill's shoulder.

"A box."

"Maybe someone's fishing minnows," said Tom Neely.

"I don't think so," Gilbert Pringler said. He tilted his head and gazed at the box through his shell-rimmed glasses. "Not in a closed box like this."

"Looks like a breadbox," said Tom. "Go ahead, Bill, open it."

Bill needed no urging. With little effort he pried up the catch. When he lifted the lid the curious boys all but banged their heads together to look inside.

"Hey, it's a quart of milk and some butter!" exclaimed Eddie.

"And five tomatoes," added Marvin.

"And a piece of Swiss cheese," finished Bill. A smile spread over his chubby face and he smacked his lips.

"It isn't Swiss," said Eddie. "It's brick."

"It's longhorn," Gilbert corrected. "It's too yellow for brick."

"Ask Marvin," suggested Tom. "He ought to know—he works for Mr. Pratt."

Marvin stooped over the box and studied the cheese. "Gilbert's right—it's longhorn."

"Okay," Bill said. "But what's it doing in the creek?"

"The creek's somebody's refrigerator," decided Heywood Brannigan, a tall, thin boy with eyebrows that slanted up in the middle. "You see," he explained, "the water's cold. Maybe fifty degrees——"

"Yeah, we know," Tom interrupted. "So stuff you put in it gets fifty degrees, too." He idly picked up a stone and flung it across the creek.

"You'd better put the box back, boys." It was Miss Phyfe, who had come down to see what was happening.

"Close it up, William. It probably belongs to some campers near by. Put it back and come. Our little picnic is ready."

There wasn't enough room at the table for everyone, so Marvin, Eddie and some of the other boys took their lunches to a spot in the shade of the mill. They sat on stone blocks that bordered the weed-hidden millrace and began to unwrap their sandwiches. Soon all were busy with their long-delayed refreshment.

Bill, whose belt size was the biggest in the class, swallowed a huge mouthful of jelly sandwich and looked critically at Tom. "What's all that sloppy purple stuff you've got on your hat?" he asked.

Tom's black eyebrows lowered over the icy glare he gave Bill. "That *stuff,* ignorant, is art. That's a high-class picture I painted with pokeberry juice. It's a boat."

Everyone looked interested, so Tom passed the decorated sailor hat around.

"The juice kind of ran," he apologized. When the hat was returned to him he put it on, then he addressed Marvin: "How soon are you and Eddie going to buy that boat you've been talking about?"

Marvin shrugged. "Soon's we get twenty dollars together."

"Might as well be twenty hundred," Eddie put in. "With me mowing lawns and him shifting groceries I figure it'll take about two years. Course if anybody here'd care to buy the biggest, meanest stag beetle in Shalerville——"

"I'll bet," said Bill, interrupting, "you'd sell it for twenty bucks. Thanks for your very generous offer."

"I've got three dollars," Tom said seriously. "Would you let me in on the boat?"

"Well . . . " Marvin glanced at Eddie.

"I've only got two and a quarter," broke in Heywood. "But I'd handle the sail most of the time—to make up."

"I've read about sailing," said Gilbert. "And I have five dollars."

Marvin looked around the munching group. Besides Eddie and himself, there were Heywood Brannigan, Gilbert Pringler, Bill Hostetter and Tom Neely. Altogether there were six. If they became partners they would all want to ride in the boat at the same time, and it would sink. But maybe together they could buy a bigger boat. . . .

"I don't know," Marvin said, undecided. "We'll think it over."

"That'd sure be fun!" remarked Heywood with deep feeling. "Tackin' north-by-nor'east, helm hard a-starboard and the deck awash with ten-foot seas! Ah-h . . . " He settled back with a banana and idly studied the wall of the mill with its boarded-up windows. "I'll bet this is the oldest old mill in the county," he mused. "Wonder who built it."

"Gilbert, you should know," Tom said. "You know about practically anything—even cheese. Who built the old mill?"

Gilbert tilted his head and wrinkled his brow. For a minute he looked very important behind his glasses, then he gave his answer. "This *is* the oldest flour mill in the county. It was built in seventeen-hundred-and-something by Shalerville's first settler, Obi . . . Oba-something Shaler. I have a book on the history of Shalerville, and there's a picture in it of the way the mill used to look. It shows a funny kind of a farm wagon and horses standing in front of the mill. On that same road that's up there now, I guess—except it was a dirt road then."

"Yeah," said Tom, not especially impressed.

"And it says in the book," Gilbert went on, "that during the Revolution the British were over on the other side of the river. They'd send raiding parties up from Camden and Philadelphia to get supplies. They were in Shalerville, and I suppose they raided this very mill—though the book didn't say they did."

"Sure," agreed Eddie. "They *must* have shot it up, right here—because it was a mill and full of flour for them to make biscuits and stuff."

"Maybe it was even a secret place where the Americans stored their guns and ammunition," suggested Heywood darkly. "Then it's for certain the British would sneak up on it and try to take it by surprise attack. And the Americans would be waiting for them."

"In ambush, of course," said Tom in a low voice. He clenched a half-eaten apple between his teeth and, stretching full-length on the ground, pointed an imaginary flintlock rifle toward the road. "Shoor," he mumbled through the apple, " 'sh a shwell flace t' hide don here. Back o' the twees——"

"These trees aren't three hundred years old, ya goof," Eddie said.

"It wasn't three hundred years ago it happened, either," Gilbert corrected.

"Bet there was fighting here anyway," declared Heywood. "Maybe there are even some old British graves around."

Marvin, so far, had not added to the discussion. Inch by inch he had been searching the wall for possible bullet holes. He wouldn't have been surprised to discover a round hole the exact size of one of the cannon balls that were stacked beside the old cannon at Ferry Street.

Suddenly he sat up straight, his scalp tingling!

Heywood saw him and frowned. "Hey, what's the matter?"

Marvin pointed to the corner window. "I just saw it move!"

"Saw what move?"

"The . . . the window—the boards on the window!"

Tom gave Marvin an odd look. "Aw, you're crazy.

How could the boards move? They're nailed down like all the rest."

"They *did* move," Marvin insisted. "They all moved at once, like a shutter. They opened just a little way and then shut again, real slow."

By now each boy was alert. All eyes were fixed on the corner window.

Then the sound of laughter came from the direction of the picnic table, and Miss Phyfe called out cheerfully, "Come, everyone! Watermelon!"

The boys by the mill, motionless as six statues, abruptly came to life and dashed for the melon. Marvin got his slice. He took a large bite from it and sat down on the bench beside Elaine Miller, who lived on a nearby farm.

Elaine moved over a little to allow room for his elbow. She glanced sideways at him. "Why were you boys holding so still over there?"

Marvin had his mouth full of watermelon. He worked his tongue back and forth until he had collected all the seeds into a pile behind his teeth. Then he flooped them out, one by one.

"Oh, nothing," he said.

"Were you just playing a silly game?"

"No. We were looking at the building."

Elaine sliced off a piece of her melon. "Why? There's nothing to look at—only stones. There's more to see inside."

Marvin considered this a moment. "Were any of the kids in there just now?"

"Oh, no. Miss Phyfe said we mustn't go in. She thinks the floor is rotten and we might have an accident."

Floop, floop, floop. Marvin shot out another load of seeds.

"And besides," Elaine continued, "I was sitting right over there where I could see if anyone went in. Why?"

Marvin changed the subject. "Have you seen any campers around this place?"

"I'm sure there aren't any. Why?"

"You live right near, and I just thought you might have seen someone."

Elaine looked at him strangely. "Why are you asking all these questions?"

"Oh, nothing."

"You said that before, Marvin Tucker. I want to know——"

Just then Miss Phyfe, who was putting things into a basket, straightened. She looked upward and her finger flew to her mouth. "Shush, children!" she warned in a loud whisper.

A thin little *zeep, zeep* came from a branch overhead.

Everyone followed her gaze, but no one saw anything.

Miss Phyfe was almost graceful as she tiptoed one

or two steps to her left. "I do believe it's a Blackburnian warbler, children! *Do* try to see it! Black head striped with orange, throat and breast orange, back and tail coverts . . . There! There! . . . Oh, dear, he's flown to the next tree!"

She jarred the whole picnic table as she turned to give chase. "Come, everyone!" she cried. "We'll get a good view!"

Nearly all of the class followed her bobbing straw hat into a thicket of elderberry bushes, where they threshed about in an effort to break through to the next tree.

Marvin, Eddie and Heywood stayed behind. Marvin hadn't finished his watermelon, bug-minded Eddie was not interested in birds that ate bugs, and Heywood had once seen this kind of bird.

Eddie thoughtfully studied the waving elderberry bushes. "You know," he said slowly, "that stuff would make first-class cover for an ambush."

"Uh-huh," agreed Heywood. He folded his long arms on his chest and thrust a foot forward. "But it's on the wrong side of the mill. The Redcoats wouldn't mess around in the back country. They'd come swaggering right up the main dirt road out of Shalerville, on the other side of the mill. So a party of Americans lying in wait on this side——"

"We get it," said Eddie.

"Say, fellows," Marvin said, "let's take a look inside the mill. Maybe we can see that corner window."

Heywood paled a little. "Miss Phyfe said not to go in."

"She didn't say it to us," reminded Eddie.

"Oh, come on," Marvin urged. "We won't go in very far. Just enough to see what's in the corner."

"Well . . . okay." Heywood, whistling softly, fol-

lowed Marvin and Eddie toward the front of the building.

"Cut the whistling," Eddie whispered, and Heywood stopped.

Now they were at the threshold of the mill. The door was open. The three investigators stopped for a minute, focusing their eyes to the darkness of the interior. Little by little they became aware of the grotesque shadowy shapes of mammoth wooden gears, columns, grinding stones, gaping storage bins and masses of strange, crouching machinery.

Heywood balanced himself as if ready for instant

flight. "Wow!" he exclaimed. "This is straight from a class-B movie thriller! First thing you know a beady-eyed, hairy monster'll come at us with slobbering jaws."

"Yeah," Eddie mumbled. "This *gets* me!"

Marvin suddenly poked Eddie's arm. "Look! In the corner!"

Eddie followed Marvin's pointing finger, and Heywood peered over their shoulders.

"A l-light!" stuttered Heywood. "L-like it's coming from under a door!"

Marvin's stomach did queer things. "It's a funny kind of light. It sort of goes up and down real fast—bright and dim and bright and dim. Do you think we could get closer?"

"We might fall over something and make a lot of noise," Eddie warned.

"And whatever's in there'll be after us," said Heywood. "Let's go back."

This was exactly what Marvin and Eddie were thinking, and so the three detectives retreated.

But Marvin wasn't satisfied. "Let's go around and see if there's another window in that corner, at the end of the mill where the junk pile is. If there is, it would be for the same room. Maybe there'd be something to stand on, and we could look in."

"Okay," said Eddie.

"It's an idea," admitted Heywood, glancing over his shoulder. "But we'll have to be quiet."

They struggled through a tangle of wild grapevines

to the end of the front wall. After they turned the corner of the building, they halted. In front of them was the sloping dump of tin cans, rusty pipes, cooking pots, and castoffs of every description. There *was* a window in the corner, boarded up, as were all the others.

Marvin studied it in relation to the lay of the junk. "I could get down there," he said, "and pile some of that stuff against the wall."

"And there are cracks between the boards on the window you could see through," said Heywood in a hushed voice. "We'll keep watch from here."

Marvin gingerly started down the slope, staying close to the wall. At one place his foot caught on a wire that pulled at a vinegar bottle which, in turn, started a small slide of cans. He froze to the wall, and Eddie and Heywood hunched into the grapevines. When all was quiet again Marvin continued downward to a place below the window. With cautious movements he rolled a dented tar barrel into position and put a box on top of it. Then, feeling for handholds on the rough stone wall, he eased himself up. He found a crack through the window boards and looked in.

At that moment the box skidded from under his feet and rolled toward the pool below. Wildly reaching for a hold on something that wasn't there, Marvin bounced off the tar barrel and crashed noisily into the rubbish.

"Be-jeeps!" exclaimed Eddie.

Heywood looked around with wide eyes. "Kind of noisy," he commented.

There was no longer any need to be secretive, for Marvin's accident had started another slide. It was a big one. Dozens of objects bounced, skittered, banged, thumped and thudded on their way to the pool.

Marvin sat quietly until he had a chance to get up. He rose and tried to start back. But his right foot had become wedged between the bars of the headpiece of a brass bed, and he couldn't get it out. He tugged and twisted and pushed and pried, but the bed held as firmly as a bear trap.

"You stuck?" Eddie called.

Marvin sat down. "I guess so," he said.

Eddie and Heywood began to make their way over the dump. When they were halfway down, Bill Hostetter appeared through the grapevines and looked over the scene.

"Hey," he called. "What're you looking for?"

"Marvin's stuck," explained Eddie. "Did you find that bird?"

"Yeah, but it gave us a hard chase."

"How far up did you go?" asked Heywood.

"Up to the fishing hole."

"The fishing hole?" repeated Eddie with interest. "Say, let's all go up there tomorrow afternoon. Maybe we can get some big ones."

"Bernie Bumbaugh got a sucker that long," Heywood said, measuring with his hands. "Day before yesterday. And he was using jelly beans for bait. Painted eyes on 'em to look like grubs."

"Ha," scoffed Bill. "I heard of a guy once who used buttons from an old pajama top——"

"Hey!" shouted Marvin from below them. "Remember me?"

As Eddie and Heywood continued downward, a number of their classmates gathered at the top edge of the junk. There was some shouting and a lot of running back and forth. Miss Phyfe, her hat in her hand and her face red, came puffing through the vines. "Oh!" she gasped. "Boys! Come right back up! That's *no* place to play."

"We're not playing, Miss Phyfe," Heywood said. "Marvin's stuck and we're going to get him loose."

"Stuck? Oh, dear, please hurry."

Eddie and Heywood reached Marvin without mishap, but they were unable to release his foot.

"Come on down, some of you guys," Eddie called. "We'll have to carry him up, bed and all."

About eight boys launched themselves downward, slipping and sliding and sending more cans to the pool. They managed to get the bed loose from the surrounding junk and lift it enough to move upward. Marvin clutched the side bars and leaned forward, giving directions and encouragement until they reached firm ground at the top, where he and the bed were set on the ground.

While the girls fluttered around and Miss Phyfe wrung her hands and begged Marvin to keep up his courage, some of the boys found a long water pipe. Using it as a lever, they attempted to spring apart the brass bars that imprisoned Marvin's foot. The water pipe bent, but the bed held firm.

Eddie turned to Miss Phyfe. "What'll we do? We can't get him loose."

Miss Phyfe smiled with her mouth, but her eyes had a confused look. "It's all right, Edward. I'm sure everything will turn out for the best. Yes, I know it will. It always does, usually." She dabbed at her forehead with a handkerchief and smiled kindly at Marvin.

Marvin smiled back.

Then Heywood had an idea. "Let's carry him into town. We can take him to a plumber."

"I don't know," objected Eddie. "Plumbers are pretty busy, and we might have to wait a couple of days."

"Wendle's Hardware Store, then," Heywood suggested. "They're always glad to do odd jobs for people."

Miss Phyfe thought that would be splendid. "Try to get Marvin there safely," she said. "I'll stay here with those who want to finish the picnic, and later I'll inquire about him at the store."

And so Wendle's Hardware Store was the destination of the parade that immediately formed in front of the mill. Lanky Heywood Brannigan, stiffly erect with a gas-pipe baton, stood in front. A few paces behind him were four standard-bearers, each with his shirt waving on a pole. Behind them, Marvin and the bed rested on the shoulders of four husky classmates, and a rabble of noisy boys and girls brought up the rear.

When all was ready Heywood faced his followers and raised his baton. He imitated a shrill trumpet call, about-faced, then stepped forward with measured strides. Shouts, cheers and bicycle bells rang out, and the procession started for town.

Marvin swayed with the easy rhythm of his tubular platform and gazed contentedly at the scenery along the road. His foot was comfortable enough, and he was thankful for the folded sweater someone had given him for a cushion.

When they entered town Heywood signaled a slower pace. The marchers spread out across Pickett Street, and the noise from the rear became louder than ever. People began to trail along on the sidewalk. Dogs barked, and children ran out of houses and yards.

After they crossed the canal bridge Marvin saw his brother Emery, mouth open and eyes wide, in front of his house. Marvin straightened. He folded his arms with the dignity of a Chinese lord. Bowing slightly to the right and then the left, he soberly accepted the puzzled stares of his sidewalk audience. Two or three times his rhythmic motion was disturbed when one or another of his bearers got out of step. But when this happened a tap on the offender's head served to correct the error.

They turned left on River Street and started across the cement bridge over the millpond. A small, muddy, yapping dog ran up from the bank. It leaped up and down against the legs of the bed carriers with such enthusiasm that several of the boys stumbled. The bed tilted, and Marvin clutched it desperately with both hands to avoid being spilled over the bridge rail. Someone finally caught the dog, and the parade continued in an orderly way for the remainder of the march through town.

At the entrance to the hardware store Heywood made a smart right-face and strode in. The four standard-bearers lowered their shirts and followed him through the store to the service department in the rear.

Outside, the bed carriers ran into trouble. Their first attempt to get through the door resulted in some scratched paint and a bump on Marvin's head. They backed up a little, and while Marvin ducked they tried it again, going faster. This rattled things in the show window, but it didn't get them through. They backed up a second time and were ready for another run, with Marvin and the bed tilted at a steep angle, when Mr. Wendle rushed out with his hands in the air.

"That's enough! That's enough!" he shouted.

WARE
SAVE

Trembling, he spread his arms across the doorway. "What do you want? Are you trying to wreck my store? Go away . . . please!"

Eddie, who was the left-front carrier, moistened his lips. "We didn't want to wreck anything, Mr. Wendle. We have an odd job we though you could——"

Just then one of the standard-bearers came back through the store to see what had held up the rest of the parade. His shirt, swinging on its pole, brushed the back of Mr. Wendle's head. The storekeeper whirled around. Then he dashed through the crowd, shouting that he was surrounded.

Marvin watched him go. "Guess he doesn't want our business."

"Come on, fellows," said Eddie. "Let's go to a plumber."

They were turning around when Heywood came out and stopped them. "I found one of the clerks in the service room," he said, "and I told him what we wanted."

The clerk, grinning broadly, came through the door with a hacksaw and a crowbar. In a few minutes Marvin was free.

The clerk carried the brass bed away, the standard-bearers put on their shirts, and the crowd began to thin out.

Marvin sat on the curb and rubbed his ankle.

"You going back to the picnic with us?" Eddie asked.

"I've got a sore foot," said Marvin. "You go ahead."

"Okay. I'll bring back your bike."

When Eddie and the others had gone, Emery—who had joined the parade—sat down beside his brother. "You sure looked good coming down the street that way," he said with admiration. "How'd you get stuck?"

"Just fell in a junk pile." Marvin got up and tested his ankle. "I was looking through a window."

"Junk piles don't have windows."

Marvin was thoughtful a moment. "It was a window in the old mill," he confided. "If you'll take my grocery deliveries tomorrow morning, I might tell you what I saw."

Chapter 3

Bugs, Boats and Tattoos

IN FRONT of their house the next morning Emery eyed his brother suspiciously. "How do I know what you saw through the window is going to be worth my slaving all morning?" he asked. "I was going to work on my soap-box racer."

"It'll be worth it, all right. It's something very mysterious." Marvin was eager to be off to the Van Trant estate and his banana spider. "Go ahead, Emery. Right hand up and hope to die a-lingerin' if it isn't worth it. It'll be okay with Mr. Pratt, and you'll only have to make about five deliveries."

Emery looked at the scuff on his shoe. "Give me your lucky nickel first. If what you saw turns out all right, I'll give it back."

Marvin scowled, but he reached in his pocket for the nickel—one that had been flattened on a railroad track. He gave it to Emery. "Now beat it. I'll see you at lunch."

As Emery left, a bicycle rumbled the boards on the bridge, and a moment later Eddie braked to a stop beside Marvin. A cardboard box with holes in the lid was in his handle-bar basket, and a homemade butterfly net was stuck through the wire.

"All set?" Eddie asked.

"Yes, soon's I get my net."

In five minutes they had left the town behind and were on the three-mile stretch down River Road to the Van Trant estate. On their right a steep bank of underbrush crowded the road. Close to them on the left was the abandoned canal and beyond that the broad Delaware River. The river, patterned with glistening ripples, rounded a gentle bend a little farther on where the red-brick chimney of the cement-bag factory cut into the sky. They could glimpse from here the upper tip of Locust Island, like the prow of a bright-green ship coming around the bend. It was a beautiful day, but Marvin and Eddie were hardly aware of it.

"I've been thinking about those groceries we found

in the creek," remarked Eddie. "Do you suppose they really belonged to campers, like Miss Phyfe said? I didn't know anyone ever camped around there."

"No," said Marvin, "no one does. Elaine Miller told me."

"Well, then, who—?"

"I've sort of got it figured out," Marvin went on. "Just before the box I was standing on fell, I got a quick look through that window."

"Did you see anything suspicious or . . . or uncanny?"

"I sure did. It was a little room, lighted by that funny glow. It wasn't very bright, but I noticed a couple of things. There was a flashlight on a table and a big round shadow moving on the wall. Like the shadow of a head—a gorilla's head, maybe."

Eddie's eyes grew large. "Golly!" he breathed.

"And that wasn't all," continued Marvin. "There was a noise that sounded like scratching, or like something heavy being jerked across the floor."

In spite of the familiar landscape and the patchwork of sunlight on the road Eddie felt a shiver run up his back. Marvin, too, now that he thought again of that corner room, suddenly felt a bit chilly.

After a minute of silence Eddie spoke. "Gorillas don't keep their butter in a creek."

"Well . . . maybe it was a man."

Eddie thought this over. "That mill's a swell hideout. . . . Say! Let's go down to the post office when we get back and take a good look at the pictures of criminals."

"Okay, that's a super idea!" Marvin was enthusiastic. "We could study them and read about where to look for scars and tattoos."

"Sometimes they've got fingers missing," Eddie added.

Marvin nodded. "Probably blown off with nitroglycerin, opening bank safes."

"Yeah, that's powerful stuff. Dangerous, too—you've got to handle it like it was TNT."

They rode on awhile without talking. Ahead of them was the public park at the historic place where Washington had crossed the Delaware. But before they came to it they turned onto a dirt road which was traced by the white rail fence of the Van Trant estate.

"Tell you what," said Marvin. "When we get back, and after we check the post-office pictures, we can plan a secret expedition to go out to the mill. We can lie in wait for whoever is hiding there—we might get a good look at him."

"Or even capture him if there's enough of us," said Eddie excitedly. "Maybe there'd be a huge reward, and we could buy a whopping big boat that all of us could get into at once. Sure, let's do it!"

They had come now to the main gate in the fence. They passed through it and pedaled a short distance up the driveway. Through the foliage of maples and evergreens Marvin and Eddie could see the house ahead. But here by the drive was the lily pond, rock-bound and bordered with flaming orange azaleas and thick-leaved rhododendrons. Its possibilities quickened the hearts of the bug collectors. This was new water to be explored. The spider could wait.

They laid their bikes on the grass and trotted over to the edge of the pond with their nets and box. Instantly they spotted ten or more water beetles that were making circular trails by a lily pad.

"They're brown ones," said Marvin. "Got any of those?"

"No, I haven't. They're all black down at the creek." Eddie leaned over the water and swished his net at the beetles. He caught four, which he picked out of the net and put into the box.

"Two for me?" asked Marvin. "I'll need brown ones, too."

"Sure. Let's see what else there is."

They moved slowly along the bank. It was a bug hunter's paradise. They collected a great many moisture-loving insects which one or the other wanted for his collection. Their prize catches were a pair of blue-winged dragonflies and four peculiar bugs with spotted heads.

When they had completely encircled the pond the boys took one last close look at the water's edge. Kneeling, with their faces near the water, they were so intent they didn't notice the car that came through the gate and rolled to a stop by the pond.

Mrs. Van Trant stalled the motor and studied the twin pairs of upended blue jeans. Then she coughed.

The boys scrambled to their feet, and Eddie wiped some water from his nose.

"Oh, hello, Mrs. Van Trant." Marvin smiled. "You've . . . you've got a lot of good bugs."

"He means here," said Eddie.

"Yes," Marvin added. "Around the pond."

Mrs. Van Trant saw the long-handled nets and laughed. "I suppose, Marvin, that you have come for the spider."

"That's right, we did. Is it . . . do you still have it?"

"Oh, yes, indeed! At least, I hope so. My brother took charge of it. He thought it was quite an animal."

She motioned toward the rear door of the car. "Hop in. We'll go up to the house and I'll get it for you."

Marvin and Eddie got in with their nets and the box and closed the door. A minute's ride up the winding driveway brought them to the big old Pennsylvania Dutch farmhouse. It was a stone building which had been restored with careful attention to original detail—even to the hand-wrought iron knocker on the door and the wavy bubbled glass in the small windowpanes.

Mrs. Van Trant stopped by the entrance and all got out.

"Come in, boys," she invited, going up the steps. "You may wait in the front hall. I'll only be a few minutes."

Inside, she disappeared through a room to the right of the hall.

The boys stood beneath a huge star-shaped lamp that hung from the ceiling. Against the paneled walls were a sofa, several antique ladder-back chairs and a slender-legged cherry stand, upon which were a number of plaster figures of deer and other animals.

"Gee," murmured Eddie, looking around, "what a place!"

"Shh-h," Marvin whispered. "Listen."

Someone had come into the room that was just out of sight on the left of the hall. A man was talking: "I tell you I've searched just about everywhere—walls, ceiling, floor. It's gone, that's all."

"It's very strange that it should disappear like that," said another man. "Are you sure you looked well?"

"Fine-toothcombed the place."

Marvin looked at Eddie. "Now they've gone and let it get away," he whispered. "The biggest doggoned spider I ever saw."

The first man's voice continued: "I suppose I should give it another try, but I'm pretty worn out and I don't enjoy getting spider webs all over my face."

"Good night!" whispered Eddie. "They've sure enough lost her. Maybe we could help them hunt."

Just then Mrs. Van Trant returned. In her hand was the mayonnaise jar, with the huge black spider crouched on the bottom!

"Gee, you found it!" Marvin grinned, taking it from her. "Guess you'd better tell your brother. He's still looking——"

Suddenly Mrs. Van Trant screamed and tore at her hair. "Get it out! Take it away!" She bent over double, and bobby pins scattered on the floor while she continued to scream and shake her head.

The boys' eyes nearly popped.

"Golly, Mrs. Van Trant," Marvin said, "it didn't get out. Anyway, banana spiders don't bite . . . I think."

"Take it away!" cried Mrs. Van Trant.

Two men rushed from the room on the left. One of them, to the surprise of the boys, was Mr. Ziggley, the mayor. The other, a tall man with a mustache, grabbed Mrs. Van Trant by the shoulders and straightened her up.

"Sarah!" he said. "What on earth? *Sarah!*"

Marvin loudly cleared his throat. "It's all right, mister. She found the spider and we're taking it home right away. You won't have to look any more." He glanced at Mrs. Van Trant, who was still shaking her head. Then he took Eddie's arm. "Come on, Eddie, let's go."

"Just a minute," said the man. He turned to the mayor. "Don't let them out till I find what's wrong.... Now, then, Sarah, what is it?"

"My . . . my hair," stammered Mrs. Van Trant. "Something big flew into my hair! I . . . I think it was a bat!"

"Let me see," said the man. He searched through the tangle a moment. "Aha! Here it is."

He pulled out a dragonfly. The insect, with a bent wing and as exhausted as Mrs. Van Trant, rested quietly in the palm of his hand. He offered it to Eddie.

"This yours?" he asked.

Eddie looked at the box he had been squeezing under his arm and noticed that the lid had opened a little.

"Yes," he said, taking the dragonfly. "Thank you very much."

Mrs. Van Trant shrieked again, pointed to the plaster figures on the stand, and fell back into the man's arms.

One of the spotted-head bugs was crawling along the nose of a deer, but Marvin quickly captured it. The man led Mrs. Van Trant to the sofa, patting her arm

and promising her something cold for her forehead.

He nodded toward Marvin and Eddie. "Take a look around, boys, to see if any others got out of your box. Then suppose we step outside." He went down the hall for something cold.

Only one more bug was found—a water beetle trying to swim on the rug. The boys and Mr. Ziggley went out of the house.

The mayor, a short, stout, bushy-eyebrowed man who wore glasses fastened to a black ribbon, spoke for the first time. "Mrs. Van Trant can tolerate insects in moderation——"

"We——" Marvin began.

"But not *loose* ones," finished the mayor.

"We——" said Eddie.

"Her brother and I were discussing some business," Mr. Ziggley went on.

"We——" said Eddie again.

"And this . . . this toodledoo with bugs is wasting our time."

"We're sorry. We'll be going now," said Eddie real fast.

"Umm . . . yes," murmured the mayor. "Time is a precious gift, not to be . . . er . . . frittered. Frittering wastes time."

When the boys turned to go Mrs. Van Trant's brother came to the door. He winked at them and announced, "She'll revive pretty soon. She needed the rest, anyway."

"Yes," said Marvin. "Good-by, and thanks for taking care of my spider."

"I didn't mind a bit. And I gave it two flies for dinner. Well, come back any time. There's a swamp in the back pasture where there are plenty of specimens." He waved good-by and went into the house with Mr. Ziggley.

The boys—with their nets, the box and the spider—walked down the driveway to their bicycles.

"Mrs. Van Trant's brother's a nice guy," remarked Marvin as they wheeled side by side through the gate. "Wonder what his business with the mayor is."

"I don't know, but it must be something important. Mayors can't fritter around unless it's something important." Eddie thought a moment. "What do mayors do?" he asked.

"Oh, they do lots of things—like making speeches on the Fourth of July, and wearing black coats and cutting ribbons across bridges, and keeping law and order all over town."

This mention of law and order brought up the next business on hand—the secret expedition to the old mill. For the next two-and-a-half miles they discussed it, and by the time they reached the outskirts of Shalerville they had agreed on a bold and dangerous plan.

Thinking of the reward money they might soon possess, they turned off the road and bumped down the lane to Old Cappy's boatyard. The aged captain was not in the weather-grayed shed where he kept his supplies, so they began a search for him outside.

The "yard" was an expanse of cleared ground beside a canal inlet from the river. Scattered about the area were a great many boats—canoes, launches, rowboats, sailing craft and a number of odd hulks—and most of them in need of paint and repairs. It was usually fun to prowl among these time-scarred relics of the river. But today Marvin and Eddie were in a hurry.

"Do you suppose Cappy's gone?" asked Marvin after they had looked around.

"He's always here." Eddie cupped his hands to his mouth and shouted, "Hey, Cappy!"

A near-by rowboat that was propped upside down suddenly slid off its props, revealing a white-bearded old man in tar-stained dungarees and a striped sweater. He rubbed his head and mumbled something under his breath. Finally he looked up.

"Ahoy!" he said.

"Ahoy, Cappy!" answered Marvin. "We'd like to look at some boats. Do you have any sailing vessels for sale?"

Old Cappy got up slowly and squinted at the boys through wispy eyebrows. "Did ye change yer minds about riggin' a sail on a rowboat?"

"Some other fellows are joining up with us," Eddie explained, "and we'll need something bigger."

"Maybe a seven-seater," said Marvin.

The old captain looked around the yard and shook his head. "Nothin' that big what sails," he said. "I've got some six-seaters ye could rig a sail to. Course those are old shad-fishin' outfits, and they'll smell like shad till their stitches bust. Ye fixin' to do some fishin'?"

"Not exactly," said Eddie. "We just wanted to explore along the river."

Marvin's gaze had been wandering over the boats in the yard. Suddenly he saw something that made him catch his breath—a large, square-ended flatboat with a low cabin in the bow. It was one of the old canal barges that had been hauled by mules plodding along the towpath many years before he was born. The

old barge lay in the still water of the inlet, pretty as a calendar picture with its clean blue sides, the white forward cabin and the glistening gray paint on its deck. It was the answer to his dream of adventure.

He nudged Eddie and nodded in the canalboat's direction. Eddie looked. His eyes brightened and he returned the nod with vigor.

"Say, Cappy," Marvin said, trying hard to keep his voice level, "there's an old tumble-down thing over there. Sort of looks like it's not much good any more—

seems to be what's left of a leaky old beat-up canal barge. How much would you sell it for, in case somebody should want it? For the wood, maybe?"

Cappy put his hands behind his back and looked at the sky. "Well," he drawled, "I'd sell that scuttled old split-seamed, bilge-bottomed scow for two hunnerd dollars . . . case a body'd want it."

"But . . . but . . . " Marvin wondered what the reward for a captured criminal would be. Maybe only fifty dollars or so.

"She's as good as new, matey," the old captain went on. "Fresh planks in 'er bottom, new hardwood roof on the cabin, caulked 'n painted t' the rails. She don't want nothin' but the motor to make 'er go, and I'll get that on pretty soon."

"Oh," said Marvin, "I didn't know you'd fixed it. How much would a six-seater shad boat be?"

" 'Bout forty-five." Old Cappy's eyes crinkled. "I know you young fellers'd have yourselves a mighty good time a-pushin' that barge about, and it'd do my heart good t' see 'er in your command. But truth is I've put a smart deal o' money in 'er, and the engine alone—secondhand—is a good part of that price."

"Well, thanks anyway," Marvin said. "I guess we'll be back later and get one of the shad boats. Maybe we could put a sail on it."

"A sail'd cut down yer passenger list," said Cappy.

"We'll take turns," Eddie suggested.

"Sure," said Marvin. "We'll have a lot of fun with it."

They said good-by to Cappy, and after a last yearning look at the barge they steered their bikes toward home.

Early in the afternoon they met again and went uptown to the post office.

They were accustomed, on their infrequent stamp-window errands, to linger beneath the wall painting at one end of the lobby. It was a colorful mural of George Washington's famous crossing of the Delaware—a picture of rough water, jagged ice, grim-faced men and the sturdy, courageous figure of the general in his windblown cape. But today Marvin and Eddie had eyes only for the bulletin board.

Thumbtacked among overlapping rummage and bake-sale announcements were six "Wanted" notices. Each bore the profile and full-face photos of a criminal, with a description and other information below.

Without a word, both boys began to read.

At length Marvin asked, "Which one do you think he is?"

Eddie rubbed the back of his stubble haircut. "Well, it's kind of hard to decide, but my guess would be case number 98076-F—Wismer Woolsey, alias Willie

Woodley. He's head of a gang, and they robbed a mail truck."

Marvin looked at Mr. Woolsey's long nose and the bald spot on his head. Then he reread a little of the information, including the part about one of his ear lobes being cut off in a fight.

"Nope," he decided.

"Why not?" asked Eddie. "His home address is in Camden, and that's real close. He might have been in Shalerville before and known about the mill."

"That's just it," argued Marvin. "Nobody who commits a crime ever stays anywhere near where he committed it. He gets as far away from the committing place as he can to hide out."

"Maybe you're right," Eddie admitted. "Which do you think it is?"

Without hesitation Marvin pointed to the picture of a hard-faced man with droopy eyelids and a mean expression.

" 'Case number 60499-D'," he read, " 'Heinie Smitszywiecs. Age forty-three, height five feet eight inches, weight one hundred and fifty to one hundred and seventy pounds. Complexion dark, hair black, large mustache—may have been shaved off. Former home Portland, Oregon.

" 'Marks—indented scar above nostril, right side; scar cut—right eyebrow, outer corner. Tattoos—mermaid and rose garland, left forearm; frigate *Constitution* and 'Don't give up ship,' right forearm.

" 'Violation—Using mails in sale of worthless antifreeze solution, defrauding number of filling stations and garages. Also sells ball-point pens through fraudulent use of mails.' "

"Sounds good," admitted Eddie. "But why—?"

"Look," said Marvin, "he lived in Oregon. Shalerville is about as far away from there as you can get. So naturally this is where he'd come."

"Yeah," Eddie agreed. "That's right! And he could be heading for New York, which is a big city, and just be laying low here until they stop looking for him."

"Of course!"

"He probably jumped off a freight train up at the station, and saw that this was a little place and it wouldn't have a police department."

Marvin nodded. "That's right. Then he walked up the road and saw an old mill that no one was using, and . . . well, there he is!"

"Say!" Eddie's eyes grew big. "I'll bet he's the guy who hit the cashier on the head and robbed that super market up River Road the other night! He'd need money if he was going on to New York. And those groceries in the creek——"

"Yeah, the groceries! . . . We ought to check them for labels." Marvin looked again at the notice. "Boy! One thousand dollars reward! That's enough for a whole fleet of boats. Come on! Let's round up our raiding party!"

Excitedly they pushed open the post-office door and hurried along Bridge Street.

Turning in the direction of Heywood Brannigan's, Marvin asked, "Remember the criminal's name?"

"Smitsy-wicks," said Eddie. "Gosh! I can hardly wait to see that picture of the *Constitution* on his arm!"

Chapter 4

Smitsy-wicks

At eleven o'clock the following morning Marvin and six other boys, some carrying oddly shaped bundles, strolled along the road toward the old Shaler Mill. In casual groups of two and three they straggled from one side of the road to the other, making an elaborate show of studying weeds at the roadside or of picking up stones to fling down the bank toward the creek. Occasionally, on Marvin's signal, two of the boys went through the motions of a friendly tussle, rolling over a couple of times on the ground, then getting up to chase after the others.

Once they heard a car approaching from the direction of the mill. Instantly Marvin whistled. The seven boys scattered to the roadsides and flattened themselves in the underbrush. The car came and passed. It was Elaine Miller's father in his aged sedan. When he was well out of sight, Marvin whistled again and the boys reappeared to continue on their way.

At last they came to a place where they could see the stone gable of the mill. Another whistle from Marvin sent everyone scooting into the dense foliage of sumac and small crab-apple trees at the left of the road.

From there they went ahead single file until they arrived at a point directly opposite the dark gaping doorway of the mill. They tossed down their bundles and squatted in a circle. Then Marvin explained in a low voice the details of his plan.

"First," he said, "there's plenty of time. Smitsy-wicks—that'll be our code name for the criminal——"

"That *is* his name," said Eddie. "Unless he turns out to be some other crook."

Marvin gave him a frown and went on: "The Smitsy-wicks won't come out until lunchtime. We'll know when that is because we'll hear the bag factory's twelve-o'clock whistle."

"How do we know he'll come out?" asked Tom Neely.

Heywood arched his eyebrows at him. "He keeps his lunch in the creek."

"Now," went on Marvin, "I'll go down first and look in the door to see if there's any light in the corner room. If there is that means the Smitsy-wicks is in there. I'll signal—one owl hoot—and then I'll crouch against the wall just outside the door. Got that?"

"Yeah," said the others in chorus.

"Okay. Then, Bill, you put on your tan overcoat and your father's old hat and work your way around to the back of the mill. Get behind one of the rocks near the Smitsy-wicks' lunch. Your coat and hat are the same color as the rocks, so you'll look like one. Your job is to signal us—two owl hoots—if he comes out a back way. Let us know when you're in position—give three hoots. That clear?"

"Two hoots and three hoots," repeated Bill solemnly.

"Third stage," Marvin continued: "Eddie comes down with his butterfly net—I'll have mine—and he takes his position on the other side of the door from me. When he's set he'll hoot four times. Then, fourth stage: Heywood and Tom will come to the doorway. Heywood stands behind Eddie, and Tom behind me. They'll bring their ropes and give five hoots."

"That's a lot of hooting," said Emery, who had talked Marvin into letting him come.

"Can't be helped," Marvin answered. "If we start using miaows and whistles and wolf howls we'll get all mixed up."

"Yeah, I suppose," Emery agreed. "Go on—what's stage five?"

"That's you, Emery. You're the trigger man."

Emery half stood up. *"Trigger man?* Hey, I quit right now!"

"Aw, sit down. What I mean is, you're the one who sort of pulls the trigger for the whole plan. It's a very super-important job, and everything depends on you. You're the shortest one here and that's why——"

Just then they heard a car coming down the road. Though they were well screened from view, all seven boys fell flat on their stomachs. It was Mr. Miller returning from town. When he had passed, Marvin whistled and the council of strategy continued.

"What do I do?" Emery asked.

Marvin opened one of the bundles and took out a girl's dress and a bright-yellow Halloween wig.

Emery gawked at the dress and started to get up again. "Oh, no, you don't!"

"You want to help catch the Smitsy-wicks, don't you?"

"Well . . . yes, but——"

"Understand, catching desperate men isn't easy. We all have to do stuff we don't like, even when it hurts us to the core. You've got to suffer."

Emery was silent.

Marvin continued his outline of stage five. "I went to a lot of trouble to get this outfit from Marybell Cruthers, and it has to be used. Now, listen. You're a little girl and you're going to be playing house or something beside the road just across from the door of the

mill. If the Smitsy-wicks should happen to see you, he won't be suspicious. He'll just think you're a little girl playing house. So you keep your eye on the door, and the minute you see him coming you start to holler like you hurt your finger. That'll be the trigger signal, and we'll take care of what happens next."

He took a small doll from the package and handed it with the dress and the wig to Emery. Scowling, Emery rolled up his shirt sleeves and the legs of his pants and started getting into the dress.

"Say, Marvin," said Gilbert Pringle, who had listened gravely to this long list of instructions, "what do I do?"

"You," answered Marvin, "are the final last emergency."

"What's that?"

"Your position is right here, where you can get a good view of everything. You keep check on each agent. If anything goes wrong, you hoot seven times and run like sixty into town and bring back the constable. He hangs out at the fire station."

"I understand," said Gilbert.

Marvin looked deeply into each of the surrounding faces. "Any questions?"

"What do you and the others at the doorway do when Emery hollers?" asked Bill.

"When you hear him, come running around to the front and you'll see. We practiced it yesterday."

"It better be good!"

"We got it down slick," Marvin assured. "Like clockwork. . . . Now does everybody know the code word?"

"Smitsy-wicks" came the chorus.

"Good. I'll go down now and check on the corner room."

Excitement stirred the huddled group as Marvin, with his long-handled net in hand, advanced to the edge of the foliage. He looked up and down the road, then dashed across it to the mill entrance. With his back pressed tightly against the wall, he stood rigid for a full half minute. Then, so slowly that the tense watchers in the foliage could hardly see him move, he got close to the door, where he could peer into the dark interior. Instantly he jumped back against the wall and hooted once.

Bill Hostetter, already perspiring in the tan overcoat, pulled the hat over his eyes and slouched down to the road. He walked along it to the far end of the mill and vanished for a few seconds behind the trunk of a willow. He reappeared and scurried to another tree, and another, until he reached the rocks by the stream. There he squatted, looking very much like a large lump of sandstone. His three hoots drifted upward.

In a little while each of the boys was in position, and the wait for the twelve-o'clock whistle began.

Marvin and his three companions by the doorway shifted from one foot to the other. They kept their eyes on Emery, for they realized it was quite possible that the Smitsy-wicks might get hungry before the whistle blew. It would be a dangerous thing if he came out and caught them off their guard.

Emery, with his sash tied in front, was gloomily playing house. Between a shallow ditch and the edge of the road he had found a big stone to sit on, and he had put a little one beside it for the doll. There he sat, staring at the mill entrance and occasionally reaching out his hand to pat the doll on the head.

Marvin glared and shook his head violently at him. He made a series of jerky motions in an effort to get Emery to make his play look more real.

Emery was puzzled for a minute, but he finally grinned and reached backward for a handful of water from the ditch. With this he began to wash the doll's face, still keeping his eyes fixed on the mill. Marvin grinned back and nodded his approval.

At that moment the bag-factory whistle blew.

The four boys at the doorway snapped to attention. Marvin and Eddie raised their butterfly nets straight up over their heads. Heywood and Tom took a firmer grasp on their ropes. A branch moved slightly in the crab-apple trees, and the "rock" by the creek became motionless. Emery stood up and energetically swung the doll back and forth by its leg.

The sound of a car was heard in the distance. It came closer and closer. . . .

Frantically Marvin motioned for Emery to vanish.

But Emery only swung the doll more furiously. Just in time to avoid being seen from the road Marvin and his aides ducked behind bushes.

It was Mr. Miller going back to town. Surprised to see a strange little girl so far from any house, he slowed down. But he passed without stopping. Marvin let out his breath. The four boys stole from the bushes, then scooted behind them again. Mr. Miller had stopped and was backing up!

He halted in front of Emery and stuck his head through the car window. "You live around here, little girl?" he asked.

Emery gave the doll a swing toward town. "Shalerville," he said in a high squeaky voice.

"What's your name?"

"Emery . . . er . . ."

"Odd name for a girl—Emerier. You sure that's what 'tis?"

Emery patted his wig down tighter. "Well," he explained, "it's really not that. It's really Emma, but my mommy thinks Emerier sounds better."

Mr. Miller scratched the stubble of beard on his chin. "Yep," he said, "I guess it's purtier. . . . Don't you think your ma might be worryin' about where you're at?"

"Oh, no."

"Wouldn't you like me to drive you t' town?"

Emery shook his head. "No. I come out here all the time and play with my doll . . . maybe."

"Hmm." Mr. Miller pulled his head into the car. "Well," he said, "if that's the case, I'll be gittin' on. Good-by, Emerier."

"Good-by," squeaked Emery.

Mr. Miller let up on the clutch and the car rattled off.

Once more Marvin, Eddie, Tom and Heywood appeared from the bushes.

They were none too soon, for the minute they had returned to their positions Emery saw the figure of a man coming from the blackness of the mill interior. He dropped the doll, held one finger high in the air as though it were smashed, and let out a horrible yell. The man, shuddering a little, stopped at the doorway.

The butterfly nets crashed over his head in one-two order. Heywood's rope whipped about his middle and his arms, and Tom's flying dive got his feet.

The man went down with his face in the grass. Emery ran over and sat on his head while the others hastily tied knots in the ropes. Bill ran up from the creek, shedding his hat and coat on the way. And Gilbert, seeing that everything was under control, came across the road to lend a hand.

Marvin finished tying a knot at the man's waist and turned to check the rope at his feet. His face paled. Lying in the grass was a pair of glasses on a long black ribbon. And the only glasses like them Marvin had ever seen belonged to Mr. Ziggley, the mayor of Shalerville!

Eddie, seeing that the knots were firmly tied, ordered,

"Everybody off. We'll turn him over to see if he has any scars on his face. And we'll look for the tattoos—the mermaid and the *Constitution.*"

Marvin found his voice at last. "Wait," he said hoarsely. "We'd better untie the ropes. I . . . I think it's Mr. Ziggley."

"Mr. Ziggley!" gasped the others.

"Yes," said Marvin. "Get off his head, Emery."

It *was* Mr. Ziggley.

The mayor sat up and spat out grass, while the boys fumbled at the knots.

Just as the last rope fell off, a voice came from the doorway of the mill: "Who are your playmates, Harold?"

The seven boys swung around as one, and Eddie made a move toward his butterfly net.

It was Mrs. Van Trant's brother! He was wearing an old shirt and overalls, and he wiped a smudge of spider web from his cheek as he looked at the astonished group.

"What is it?" he asked. "Another picnic? Or could it be that convention of diurnal owls we heard gathering out here?"

"Oh, no," said Eddie, his voice higher than usual.

"No," Marvin said, "we aren't owls."

"We're people," explained Emery.

The tall man in the doorway looked down at the mayor, who was still seated on the ground and rubbing his arms.

"You should have worn old clothes as I suggested," he chided.

Mr. Ziggley's face, already red, became redder. A clover leaf dangled from one eyebrow, and he sputtered like a frying pan as he reached for his glasses. "These . . . these rascals! Unprincipled, blundering, blockheaded whippersnappers! I'll . . . I'll . . ." Unable to continue, he rose stiffly and began to dust his pants with such force that the sound of it echoed through the mill.

His companion recognized Marvin and Eddie. "Better tell me what it's about," he said. "It isn't natural for a man like my friend Mr. Ziggley to say such things without reason. What are you boys up to?" He looked at the two nets on the ground, then asked, "Hunting bugs?" Then he saw the ropes and added, "Or what?"

"No. Not bugs," Marvin said. "We came here to capture a Smitsy with scoots and tar—scars and tattoots."

"Oh, I see."

"And it almost worked. Except . . ."

"Except?"

"It was Mr. Ziggley instead."

"And Mr. Ziggley doesn't have scars and tattoots? He's not a Smitsy?"

Marvin wished he could be far away.

The man smiled and patted him on the shoulder. "Next time, perhaps you should ask first if a person has scars and *tattoos*. And *then* net him—if he says yes, of course."

Mr. Ziggley, finished with his brushing, now drew out a large handkerchief and began to mop his face.

"Just what," he demanded, "made you think I was a . . . a Smitsy?"

"That's a criminal," said Eddie, embarrassed. "We don't think *you* are. But when we had our picnic we saw the shutter on the window move and we saw a light, and Marvin saw someone's shadow. So we thought there was someone hiding out in the mill, and——"

"Say," Marvin interrupted suddenly, "maybe you and Mrs. Van Trant's brother were looking for the same criminal we were."

The tall man smiled. "We were looking for something all right, but not for a person. And by the way, you needn't bother to call me 'Mrs. Van Trant's brother.' My name is Shaler—Robert Shaler. My sister's maiden name was Shaler too, of course."

The boys looked surprised.

Gilbert, his eyes growing big behind his glasses, asked, "Then . . . then does the mill belong to you?"

"Let's all go over to the picnic table and sit down, while I tell you the whole story," suggested Mr. Shaler. "We may as well make ourselves comfortable."

After they were settled around the table, Mr. Shaler went on: "Yes, the mill still belongs to the Shaler family. My ancestor, Obadiah Shaler, built it in 1760, and it was operated by several generations of Shalers after him. In my grandfather's time it closed down. But we've kept the building in fair condition ever since—new roof and boarded windows—thinking that someday the place could be given to the people of Shalerville as a sort of historical reminder of the early days. And that, boys, is why Mr. Ziggley and I are here. My sister and I thought it was time to transfer the property to the town."

"Gee, that's swell, Mr. Shaler!" said Marvin.

"Sure is," agreed Eddie. "But what about that corner room and the food in the creek? Hasn't someone been living here?"

Mr. Shaler chuckled and glanced toward the stream.

"Well, not exactly living here. You see, before transferring the mill we wanted to locate some of Obadiah's papers which, according to old family letters, were kept somewhere in the mill building. As far as we know they've never been found, and so they must still be here."

"But the box in the creek—?" Heywood began.

Mr. Shaler held up a hand and went on: "So I came up from Philadelphia to have a final look. I'm staying at the Van Trants', but since I spend so much time poking around the mill, I fixed up the mill office a little—with an oil lamp and a few other things."

"The flickering light!" blurted Marvin, understanding at last.

"Yes, it flickers. I used it mostly when I stayed evenings or when I needed light in the dark corners. I usually kept the window shutter open. But when you kids came romping around for a picnic, I was tearing up floorboards and didn't want to be disturbed. So I closed the shutter."

"Oh," said Tom. "And you kept the tin box in the creek . . ."

"Never knew how long I'd be here." Mr. Shaler smiled. "So I was always prepared." During most of his explanation he had been gazing idly at Emery. Now he was frankly puzzled, and he addressed him. "That's pretty yellow hair you have, little girl. Nice and thick . . . like yarn."

Emery blushed for the first time in his life. He pushed the wig off and it fell to the ground.

"Hmm," said Mr. Shaler. "An important part of the 'plan,' I suppose."

Standing up, Emery untied the sash and struggled to pull the dress over his head. It got stuck, and it took a minute or two for the others to free him.

While he unrolled his pants legs Emery frowned at the crumpled dress. "Next time," he grumbled, "I'm going to be a little boy playing Indian."

Slowly dawning on Marvin was the real meaning of the men's conversation he and Eddie had overheard in the Van Trant house. Mr. Shaler had not lost the spider at all. He had been talking about his search in the mill. Spider webs in his face . . .

A car stopped in front of the mill.

"Great hoppers!" cried Heywood. "Mr. Miller *again?*"

Mr. Ziggley rose and peered toward the road. "It's Mrs. Van Trant. She's come to pick us up, thanks be! Hardest day I've had since . . . since . . . well, since . . . since . . ."

Mrs. Van Trant beeped the horn.

"Coming!" shouted Mr. Shaler. "I think," he said to the boys, "we'll give up the search for Obadiah's papers and get started on a cleanup job in a few days. If you boys would like to help, it would be worth thirty dollars to me. How about it?"

The smile on each boy's face was answer enough.

"Just let us know when we can begin," said Eddie, "and we'll have the place cleaned up so fast you'll be surprised."

"Sure, we'd be glad to help," said Marvin. "And . . . and, Mr. Ziggley, I'm awful sorry about what . . . I mean, about how . . . "

"That's . . . er, quite all right," said the mayor, rubbing his head. "But I do think it was a considerable waste of time. Frittering. Now, something constructive, perhaps——"

"But the reward would have been a thousand dollars," objected Eddie.

"Umm, yes," muttered the mayor. "Well, Bob—" he turned to Mr. Shaler—"we're keeping your sister waiting."

The seven boys had plenty to talk about on the way home. Thirty dollars was a sizable comedown from the expected thousand for the capture of Mr. Smitszywiecs. But added to what they all had saved, it probably would be enough for a six-seater shad-fishing boat.

Chapter 5

The Hidden Door

THE cleanup at Shaler's Mill began a few days later. As soon as workmen had removed the boards from the windows, the boys attacked the brightened interior with buckets and brooms. They swept from one end to the other. Like a detail of army ants, they picked the floor clean of the dusty debris of many decades.

They cut weeds and pruned grapevines the next day. After that they began work on the junk pile. They nailed a series of planks end-to-end down the middle of the slope and made a smooth track for a large wooden box which they slid up and down on a rope. With three boys assigned to load the box, one to keep it on the track, and three to haul it up and empty it, they made rapid progress. By the end of the first afternoon the pile at the roadside, waiting for a truck, had become enormous. But the boys still had not reached the bottom of the dump. It was deeper than it had seemed, so work on it was continued to the following day.

Marvin, who spent the next morning delivering groceries, arrived early in the afternoon. He laid down his bicycle—at a safe distance from the rubbish—and went over to where the others were working.

"Any more brass beds?" he asked. "The clerk at Wendle's Hardware Store stopped in Pratt's this morning and paid me two dollars for bringing him that one."

"Two dollars?" repeated Eddie in surprise.

"Yeah. He sold it to the junk-yard man across the river. Says there's money in brass if you get enough of it."

"Gee," said Heywood, "there must be a lot of it here! Let's make a special pile of what we find."

"And keep an eye on the heap of stuff by the road when they load it into the truck," suggested Eddie. "Maybe we can make enough money for the barge instead of a smelly six-seater. Maybe we'd even have enough left over for some gasoline to run it."

Seven pairs of eyes sparkled at the thought. The evening before, all the boys had gone down to Old

Cappy's for a conference on boats. They had agreed on buying a six-seater shad boat. But with the barge in plain sight the decision had been a hard one to make.

Now, with a grander goal in view, they attacked the remainder of the junk pile with freshened vigor. Cans, bottles, pipes, wire and broken crocks clanked into the box that shuttled up and down the track. Marvin, working next to the stone wall of the mill, tugged mightily at a bedspring. All kinds of things had caught onto it, making it hard to get out.

"Here, we'll give a hand with that," offered Heywood. "Come on, Eddie."

The three boys struggled, and Gilbert and Bill came down to help.

"Somehow this makes me think of Marvin at the picnic," Bill said, puffing between tugs.

"Yeah!" Marvin grinned. "But this time it's the bed that's stuck instead of me."

They gave a super heave on the bedspring. It dislodged in an explosion of cans. The boys staggered backward and two sat down. After everything had settled, Marvin peered into the hole they had made beside the wall of the mill.

"Hey, fellows, come here!" he called. "Look, there's a door down there, going into the building!"

The others came to look.

"Probably goes into the basement," said Eddie. "What of it?"

Marvin shrugged. "Nothing, maybe. I just thought that since Mr. Shaler couldn't find old Obadiah's papers up above, they might be down here in the basement."

"How do you know he hasn't already searched the basement?" Heywood asked. "He could have gone down through the trap door on the first floor."

"He wouldn't have gone down *those* steps," Marvin argued. "They're so rickety they wouldn't hold up a cat."

"That's right," Gilbert said. "Let's tell him about this door. He's down at the creek talking to a man about a swimming-pool dam."

"Okay," said Marvin. He turned to the box haulers above and called, "Hey! Somebody get Mr. Shaler! We've got something to show him!"

Emery ran off and soon returned with Mr. Shaler.

"What did you find?" Mr. Shaler asked.

"A door to the basement," Marvin called back. "We thought your old papers might be down there."

Mr. Shaler seemed disinterested. "I've been through the basement," he said. "Nothing there but more gears and machinery. I put a ladder through the trap door."

Disappointed, Marvin looked again at the cellar door. "Maybe this'll take you into another part of the basement."

"Possible, possible," admitted Mr. Shaler. "Clear it out and see if you can get in."

The boys tackled the clearing job as though they were rescuing someone trapped by an avalanche. Rusty things whizzed through the air, and the box nearly burned up the track. In a short time the door was clear. They tried to open it, but the old latch had been buried in the junk pile so long that it had become scaly with rust and was completely unworkable.

"Hit the door a good one with your shoulders," called Mr. Shaler from above.

"Okay, men!" shouted Marvin. "Ready? One, two, three!"

The rotten frame splintered and the door whammed flat. All five pushers piled on top of it. A dense billow of dust curled upward and out of the opening as the boys staggered, one by one, back to fresh air.

"Wow!" exclaimed Eddie when his breath returned. "We could have pushed a little easier, I guess."

"Phooey!" said Heywood, wiping dust from his face with the inside of his cap.

One of the fascinated watchers above called down impatiently, "What are you waiting for? What's inside?"

Marvin took a deep breath and went through the opening. In a moment he returned and let his breath out.

"It's another room," he called to Mr. Shaler. "Like the office above."

Now Mr. Shaler was interested. He went down

along the shaky planks, balancing with arms outspread until he reached the excavation. The boys at the doorway stood aside and then followed him into the little cellar room.

The dusty beam of light from the doorway fell directly on a high long-legged desk against the opposite wall. In front of it was a stool. A corroded iron stove, a lamp and a rocking chair completed the furnishings.

"Gee," said Eddie, "I'll bet this was Obadiah's secret office!"

"Just what it was," said Mr. Shaler. "Probably a good place to relax when the flour dust or customers got too thick upstairs. And look, there's another door leading into the rest of the cellar, no doubt."

He walked over to it and lifted the latch. The door squeaked and opened about an inch, but banged into something on the other side.

"I suppose there's a pile of barrels against it—doubtless the reason I didn't notice the door before."

Marvin, who was not especially interested in the door, had gone over to the desk and raised the lid.

"Mr. Shaler!" he cried excitedly. "There are some papers and old books in here! Do you suppose they're what you're looking for?"

Mr. Shaler came over and looked into the desk. "Jove, I do believe they are!" he exclaimed. "Let me just take some out."

He extracted several packets of folded papers and

two brown pasteboard-bound account books. He rummaged briefly through some other things, then closed the lid.

"Suppose we retire with these to the picnic bench and have a quick look," he suggested. "You boys come along."

Everyone gladly took advantage of the offered rest, and soon they were settled at the table beneath the willow. Mr. Shaler put aside the packets and dusted the cover of one of the books.

"I don't have much idea of what's in here," he said, "though it's probably just old accounts of business transactions. Well, we'll see."

He opened the book and glanced over the first page.

"Are they accounts?" asked Marvin.

"They are," confirmed Mr. Shaler. "And they make pretty dull reading unless you're interested in prices, and the names of early settlers." He opened the other book in the middle.

"Hmm," he said, "this is more like it." Then he read: " 'Seventh December, 1776. Joseph Arnold stopped today. He tells that Gen' Washington and the Continentals are hard pressed and retreating from New Jersey in our direction. This means they may cross at the Kinnecong Ferry and others to take refuge in the county. We here may be hard pressed ourselves to give them quarter, but we shall see to that. There is much sentiment here for his cause, and no Tories.

" 'Eighth December. Much of the army has crossed today, several regiments by Kinnecong Ferry. All boats for many miles and the lumber and scantling are being collected from the Jersey side and being removed to the west bank of the river to discourage pursuit by the British and Hessians. Officers billeted at our house and soldiers of De Fermoy's regiment have put their tents in the mill yard. The First Pennsylvania Rifles are quartered at Thompson's mill at Solebury under command of Lieutenant James Monroe. Many of the men are barefooted and suffering.' "

Mr. Shaler stopped reading. "That'll have to be all for now, boys," he said, closing the book. "I've too much to do today, but I'll see that you'll all get a chance to read it later."

"Golly!" Heywood exclaimed. "George Washington and the Redcoats! Just what we were talking about the other day!"

"Lieutenant James Monroe," Gilbert commented with interest. "Didn't he get to be President?"

"He did," said Mr. Shaler, gathering up the packets. "I think this little journal is going to prove mighty important, and I have all of you to thank for it. . . . Well, back to the junk mine with you, while I find a spot for the dam."

At the end of the fourth day large bare spots had appeared at the bottom of the rubbish pile. A truck came and hauled away most of the heap by the road, and it seemed that only part of another day was needed to finish the job.

Everyone had kept a sharp lookout for brass and also solid pieces of iron, which the truck driver had told them was valuable. So they had a sizable pile ready to turn into money. Mr. Shaler gave them permission to sell whatever they found and offered to have the truck haul it to the junk dealer in Bakerstown, across the river.

When the day's work was done the weary boys took their time on the way home. As Marvin walked his bike beside Eddie he was deep in thought. The pile of brass and iron interested him.

"How much do you think we can get for the junk?" he asked.

"I don't know for sure," Eddie replied. "Maybe three hundred dollars."

"Naw," Haywood broke in. "Not that much. More

like seventy-five. You got two dollars for the bed, didn't you?"

"Yes," said Marvin. "But——"

"The pile of stuff we have is as big as fifty beds. So that makes . . . Let's see, fifty goes into seventy-five . . . one and . . . and . . . "

"Twenty-five fiftieths," said Gilbert.

"How much is twenty-five fiftieths?" asked Eddie, beginning to get a little mixed up.

"Well," Heywood answered, "twenty-five over fifty, cross out the fives, and that leaves two and zero—twenty dollars."

Eddie interrupted. "You're forgetting that Marvin's bed was only part of a bed. Maybe only a third of one when you count the footpiece and the rails. So if we have a pile of stuff as big as fifty whole beds, it'll be worth what Marvin's was worth a third of."

"Huh?" grunted Bill, completely bewildered.

"Three times twenty is sixty dollars." Gilbert announced this with an air of finality, and the others accepted his figure.

"I guess that's a lot of money just for some junk," said Marvin. "But I was hoping it'd come a little closer to two hundred dollars."

They went on in silence. In their minds the picture of the wonderful canal barge lying at anchor at Old Cappy's yard slowly faded, and in its place each saw himself waiting on shore for his turn in the shad boat.

Chapter 6

Old Brass and Iron

LATE the next afternoon there was not a can left to show where the old rubbish dump had been. The last truckload of junk had been hauled away, and the driver had promised to return for the brass and iron.

The old mill looked very different from the way it had on the day of the picnic. Windowpanes glistened, the interior was in order, and the millrace and the grounds were clear of weeds and brambles. Workmen were fixing the big wheel, and even the swimming-pool dam had been started.

The boys were sitting near the end of the mill, admiring the carefully raked slope that had been the dump, when the truck returned and rattled to a stop beside the brass and iron.

The driver, Pete Pennypacker, who was Eddie's older cousin, jumped out.

"Hop to it, boys," he said. "We're having an early dinner tonight. If two of you get up in the truck and pack the stuff tight, we can take it all in one load."

Everyone hustled, and soon the truck was filled and ready to go. Pete looked at the seven boys.

"Marvin and Eddie," he said, "you come along and sit on top of the load to see that nothing falls off. I could take two more up front with me."

Heywood and Emery climbed into the seat beside Pete, and as soon as Marvin and Eddie had mounted the load the motor roared.

"Bring our bikes into town," Marvin shouted to those who were left, and the truck was off.

When they were almost into town Heywood stuck his head through the glassless rear window and yelled above the clanking of the load, "Pete says the stuff's only worth about twenty dollars."

"Gee, is that all?" Marvin suddenly felt depressed. He had secretly hoped that their figuring last night had been 'way too low. But Pete was a trucker and he should know.

"It's the shad boat for sure," moaned Eddie. "Even with the thirty dollars Mr. Shaler paid us, it's got to be the shad boat."

The truck had now come into town. It bumped loudly over the canal bridge and slowed going down the hill past the Towpath Inn. A few people at the entrance to the inn stopped to stare curiously, and a man and a woman coming out of Ye Olde Kettle antique shop glanced idly at the truck.

Then the man pointed to it and called to someone inside the shop. When the truck was a few houses

farther down the street, Mrs. Binney, who owned the shop, came running out. She called to the boys and wildly waved her arm.

Marvin waved back and remarked to Eddie, "She seems to like me better. Maybe she's over being mad at me for busting her spinning wheel with my bike."

"It was her fault," said Eddie. "She had it practically on the street, and that's public property."

Mrs. Binney suddenly clutched at her skirt and began to run toward the truck. The man and the woman followed more slowly.

Pete halted briefly at the intersection of River Street. The rattling quieted, and Marvin vaguely heard Mrs. Binney call out again.

"Did she holler?" he asked.

"I think so," said Eddie.

The truck swung around the corner and headed toward the business section. As it clanked over the mill-pond bridge Mrs. Binney rounded the corner, her hair undone and strung out behind.

"I'll bet she wants us to stop," shouted Eddie.

"We didn't drop anything."

Nevertheless, Marvin reached a small iron pipe through the rear window and tapped Heywood on the shoulder. "Hey! Tell Pete to stop!"

The truck pulled to the curb in front of the Daisy Fruit Store and shuddered to a stop.

Pete looked back through the window. "What's the matter?" he asked. "What did we lose?"

"Mrs. Binney——" Eddie began.

"What?"

But Mrs. Binney had arrived.

Marvin leaned over the side of the truck. "Did you want something, Mrs. Binney?" he asked politely.

"My . . . my . . . yes. Wait till I . . . catch my . . . breath!"

She stood a minute, pushing up her hair, her chest heaving. Pete and the boys patiently waited.

"I have some customers," she finally said, "who

are looking for a brass bucket, and you have one on your truck." She took a deep breath and pointed to it. "I see it's very tarnished, and it's badly dented, and the handle is crooked. But would you sell it to me? It's just barely possible my customers would like it."

Marvin looked at the sky. "That bucket's near as good as new," he said. "It was at the bottom of the dump and out of the weather. And that little bit of tarnish is just protecting it. We could sell it for ten dollars."

"Ten—!" said Mrs. Binney, gasping. She saw her two customers approaching the truck. "All right. Get it out for me, please."

Marvin dug out the bucket and gave it to her.

By then, the man and the woman had reached the truck. The woman examined the bucket.

"It's not in very good condition," she said. "How much will it cost?"

"Fifteen," said Mrs. Binney. "It's a very fine bucket. Heavy brass and extremely old."

The lady opened her purse. "All right. We'll take it."

She gave Mrs. Binney the money, and Mrs. Binney pressed a ten-dollar bill into Marvin's hand.

"Can we go on, now?" asked Pete through the window. "We're having an early dinner tonight."

"Yeah, let's go," Marvin said.

Pete shifted to low gear and gunned the motor.

"Just a minute! Just a minute!" shouted the man who had come with the woman. "Hold up! There's something else on your truck I want to see."

Pete cut off the motor.

"Isn't that an andiron sticking out there?" asked the man, pointing. "Yes, it is. Could you get it out, boys?"

Marvin and Eddie tugged and twisted at the andiron.

"Early colonial," the man whispered to the woman, who had come to look. Aloud he asked, "Is there another one to match it?"

"I think there is," Eddie said.

The two boys began to search. Things clanked to the pavement, then Eddie came up with the andiron's mate. He handed it down to the man.

"Hmm," murmured the man, "rusty. How much?"

Behind the man, Mrs. Binney held up both hands and spread her fingers twice.

"Twenty dollars," said Eddie.

The man set the andirons on the sidewalk and gave Eddie the money.

"Can we go now?" asked Pete. "We're having an early——"

"I guess," Marvin answered. "No, wait!"

The man was pulling something through the sideboards of the truck. It was a pair of brass-handled fireplace tongs.

Mrs. Binney held up seven fingers.

"Seven dollars," said Eddie.

The man handed the tongs to the woman. "Keep a list," he said as he began yanking at something else.

Mr. Delancey, who owned a gift shop on Bridge Street, came and started poking at things on the other side of the truck.

"How much for this bit of junk?" he asked, holding up a little twisted piece of metal.

It was nothing Marvin could identify. He looked to Mrs. Binney for help, but she had her nose between the sideboards and couldn't see him.

"Twenty dollars," he said.

"A bargain," mumbled Mr. Delancey. "I'll just make a pile of things and figure the total."

Visitors were beginning to come into town for dinner and the evening show at the theater. In sport jackets and summer dresses they strolled in groups along River Street before gathering at the various inns and restaurants. The activity in front of the fruit store attracted many of them, and soon the truck was surrounded. A number of people elbowed to the truck and began to make more piles of things on the sidewalk and in the street.

Heywood and Emery climbed out of their seats to help Marvin and Eddie make up prices and take in the money. Pete Pennypacker went home for dinner.

Mrs. Binney backed away from the truck with a pair of bent candlesticks in her hands. Her eyes were bright.

"My, my!" she exclaimed. "A gold mine of brass and iron—nearly all of it eighteenth and nineteenth century. Where on earth did you boys find it?"

"Shaler's Mill dump," answered Marvin as a man waved an old teapot in his face and asked him how much.

Marvin took eight dollars for the teapot, then he turned to Eddie. "Maybe we ought to tell Mr. Shaler. He probably didn't know his junk was worth so much money."

"He said we could sell anything we found," Eddie reminded him.

"I know. But just the same I'm going to telephone him. Keep an eye on things while I——"

"He wouldn't be home from the mill yet. . . . Hey, wait! That's his car parked up by Pickett Street. Maybe he saw the commotion and recognized our truck."

Marvin saw Mr. Shaler hurrying through the crowd, saying "Excuse me" or "Pardon me" to everyone he bumped into. There was a look of anxiety in his eyes as though he feared there had been an accident. In a minute he arrived at the truck. His expression changed from alarm to puzzlement.

Then he laughed. "Antiques! Battered, bent and useless, but nonetheless antiques!"

"I was just going to call you," Marvin said. "We thought you might want to know about this stuff. It's really your junk and maybe you'll want some of it for the mill. Or the money——"

"I'm grateful to you," cut in Mr. Shaler. He reached into the truck and pulled out a rectangular piece of brass. It was a tarnished plaque with the word "Vigilant" in raised letters across its face.

"Hmm," he said. "The name plate of Shalerville's old fire wagon. I'll take this as my share of the junk and present it to the fire company. The rest is yours. You've all worked hard enough, long enough and speedily enough to have earned whatever it's worth."

"Gee, thanks!" Marvin grinned.

Mr. Shaler started back to his car, and the antique sale went on.

The crowd swelled, but only those near the truck knew what was going on. Traffic was stalled, and cars had to go around by Ferry Street to get through. The constable trotted back and forth at the edge of the crowd, asking people what had happened. He finally climbed part way up a telephone pole. He saw what was going on, and waved his arm and shouted, "Move on! Move on!" No one heard him, so he climbed down and went back to the fire station.

The four boys continued to dig things from the truck, though most of the antiques were gone. Little remained but twentieth-century plumbing and two thirds of a bed. At last the street lights went on. The crowd began to leave, and after a while the boys were alone with the truck.

Heywood kicked a faucet against the curb. "Guess we ought to clean up this mess," he said. "Pete'll be along and he'll want to get right over to Bakerstown. How much money do you think we made?"

"Golly," said Marvin, "how should I know? But I'll bet it's plenty!"

By the time they had tidied up the street, Pete arrived. He noted the shallow layer of junk that remained in the truck and screwed up one side of his face.

"Wouldn't think that stuff in there'd pay for enough gas to get the truck over the bridge," he said. "But let's go."

On the way to the junk yard the two boys in back counted their money and the two in front counted theirs. When the truck pulled into the yard and stopped, they totaled their sums. Altogether they had nearly two hundred and twenty dollars.

"Boy-oh-boy!" exclaimed Eddie. "Just wait'll the other fellows see this! I'll bet——"

"First thing tomorrow," Heywood broke in, "we'll go down to Old Cappy's. Won't he be surprised!"

"Yep!" Marvin grinned. "We'll just hand him two hundred dollars like it was cabbage leaves, and tell him to untie the rope, please, on . . . on the *Spider Queen.*"

Heywood twitched his nose. "On the *who*?"

"The *Spider Queen*," Marvin repeated. "Our barge has to have a name, doesn't it?"

"Sure," Emery said. "But how come—?"

"That name kind of seems right," Marvin said. "It was the black spider that led us to Mr. Shaler. Then Mr. Shaler led us to the junk pile. And the junk led us to the money to buy the boat."

"Yeah," murmured Heywood. "That smart little spider practically walked down to the boatyard and bought us the barge."

Marvin nodded, then he looked at the others uncertainly. "Of course it'll belong to all of us. I guess we ought to take a vote on the name."

Eddie grinned. "I think it's super!"

"Yeah," said Emery.

"Me, too," agreed Heywood. "And it'll *have* to be okay with the other guys—we've got them outnumbered."

Marvin smiled. "We'll have a christening before we launch her."

Pete, who had gone after the junk dealer, returned with him. The man switched on a floodlight and came over to stare gloomily at the contents of the truck. He reached into his pocket and took out a large roll of bills.

" 'Tain't worth the bother t' weigh it," he said, slowly peeling off some of the bills. "Brass 'n iron prices is no good today. Rags is better."

He handed seven one-dollar bills to Marvin, then told Pete where to unload.

Later the emptied truck rattled across the bridge into Shalerville. Not one of the boys who rode in it could remember when he had been so tired or so hungry. But hunger and weariness meant little when between the four of them they shared the dream of offshore breezes and faraway river islands.

Chapter 7

Sad-face and Flat-nose

OLD CAPPY was a very surprised man when Marvin, followed by the other boys, strode into his boat-yard the following morning and laid two hundred dollars in his hand. Puzzled, he looked from the money to the circle of eager faces.

"This is for the barge?" he asked.

"Yes," affirmed Marvin nonchalantly. "How soon will the engine be on it?" He glanced toward the barge and was a little startled to see two men already bolting a large outboard motor to its stern.

"Oh," he said, "you're having one put on now.

That's swell! We . . ." There was something in Cappy's expression that made him stop. He looked again at the two men.

One of them was tall, thin and sad-faced. The other, who was suspiciously regarding the boys through squinted eyes, was a stocky man with a flat, wide nose. They both wore neatly pressed trousers with bright shirts and suspenders, and they seemed strangely out of place in a boatyard. Marvin had never seen either of them before.

"I made a deal," Cappy said. "I traded 'em the barge for their pickup truck." His straggly eyebrows met in a troubled frown as he returned the money to Marvin. "If I'd only knowed ye was t' be here today, an' able t' pay for the vessel, I'd sure as the green tide have saved 'er for ye."

The boys' spirits had fallen so low they couldn't say a word. It was as though they had struggled to the peak of a mountain, only to encounter a landslide. The feeling was so plain that Marvin thought he heard rocks crashing about his head.

"If I'd only knowed!" Old Cappy repeated. "It'd sure give me more pleasure t' see 'er in your command than in them fellers' over there. They've got no more likin' for a water-goin' vessel than ducks got for a gravel pit." He rubbed his beard with the back of his callused hand and glared disapprovingly at the men. "Callin' the cabin a bunkhouse!"

"Well—" Marvin slowly turned to go—"I guess there's nothing to wait around for. Maybe we'll find another barge sometime."

"Sure hope ye can. But them square-nosed jobs is all gone from hereabouts. Don't rec'lect seein' no others."

"Maybe," said Bill, "you'll be getting something else that'll be almost as good, pretty soon."

Tom was doubtful. "It would have to be a seven-seater, and most motorboats or sailboats that big would cost even more than the barge. We *could* get two or three of those shad boats."

Marvin started up the lane. "Maybe," he said.

But just now he didn't feel like looking at shad boats, and he was sure that even the smell of one would make him a little sick. As he left the boatyard with the others, he looked back once more. The flat-nosed man was sitting on the rail of the *Spider Queen*, grinning at them in a way that made Marvin want to run over and push him into the inlet.

At the corner of River Street and Apple Lane a car drew up to the curb and a familiar voice hailed the boys. It was Mr. Shaler.

"I have news," he announced jovially. "The Ladies Garden Club has just adjourned a meeting at the Van Trant place, and they rendered a vote of thanks to you boys for doing such a bang-up . . . I mean, *splendid* job on the dump. They also voted that since the mill has become such an exquisite beauty spot, the rest of Shalerville is shabby by comparison."

Marvin started to say something. But Mr. Shaler held up his hand and continued. "There's a lot more. Mrs. Somebody moved that the whole town be cleaned up and beautified. Mrs. Somebody-else moved that there be a large celebration when the cleanup was finished. Then Mrs. Ziggley moved that the theme of the celebration be the early history of Shalerville, and that there should be a grand parade, speeches at the mill and a special show at the playhouse. The other ladies said it was a splendid idea. They voted 'yes' to the whole business."

By now the boys had slightly recovered from their keen disappointment at the boatyard. There was nothing to do about it. The *Spider Queen* was gone, and they had grudgingly resigned themselves to wait until another boat was available. So Mr. Shaler's news of excitement to come was welcome—it would help to fill in their period of waiting.

Marvin brightened at the thought of a special show. "What's the show going to be?" he asked.

"Don't know," replied Mr. Shaler, grinning. "But I'm glad to see you're interested."

"And a parade!" Emery exclaimed.

"What about the speeches?" Mr. Shaler looked at

each of them. "Doesn't anyone here like speeches?"

There was silence for a moment. Then Gilbert said, "Well, maybe."

"And cleanup jobs?"

This time there was no answer at all, and Mr. Shaler laughed. "I'll have to get on now," he said. "But be on your guard, and don't underestimate the Ladies Garden . . . Oh, I forgot—they voted also to change their name to Ladies *Civic and* Garden Club. I suppose changing the club's name gives them the same satisfaction as moving the furniture in their living rooms. Well, I've warned you!"

He drove on and the boys continued down the street.

"Parades and shows are okay," Tom said. He pushed his painted sailor hat over one eye and kicked at a stick on the sidewalk. "But I'm tired of cleaning dumps."

"Oh, I don't know," said Heywood. "We might find some more of those old brass and iron things."

"I don't think so," Marvin argued. "That dump by the mill was probably the oldest one around town, and that's why we got so many antiques. I guess I'm through with dumps, too."

"I wouldn't mind being in the parade," said Emery.

Marvin was scornful. "What would you do in a parade?"

"I could carry a drum in the Consolidated Elk and Eagle Band."

"Micky Rittenger does that."

"He's too little. He always quits after they've gone a block. Anyway, I could trade him something to let me do it."

Bill, who had been keeping a watchful rear guard, suddenly hollered, "Duck! Here comes a carload of women!"

Frantically the boys scattered this way and that. But there was no cover except a small peony plant in a near-by front yard, and Emery beat them all to it.

The worst happened—the car stopped. It was a station wagon full of club ladies.

Mrs. Piper, who was club president, leaned out the window and called, "Oh, boys!"

Marvin, caught in the middle of the front yard, gulped. "Hello, Mrs. Piper. It's a nice day."

"Yes, it is," she said. "How would all of you boys like to help us with a splendid program to bring renown to our town?"

"Bring what?"

"Make Shalerville the most delightful place in the valley."

"Well," Marvin said, "I guess . . . "

"That's splendid!" Mrs. Piper beamed and the other ladies smiled. "We'll get in touch with you later," she continued. "We'll all have just loads and loads of fun!"

After the ladies had driven on, the boys looked glum.

"I'll *bet* we have fun," growled Eddie. "Hauling old papers and cans!"

"Planting trees and scrubbing streets," Heywood added.

"And cutting weeds around the cannon," put in Bill.

Marvin shoved his fists deep into his pockets and stared straight ahead. "If we only had that barge," he said, "we could be on the river and down to Locust Island by tonight. And we'd stay there till this clean-up business blows over."

Eddie wistfully nodded his approval. "We'd come back just in time for the parade and the special show."

"Where are your consciences?" Gilbert asked. "You want the frosting without having to eat the cake."

Bill frowned at him. "Conscience," he muttered. "Now you've gone and ruined everything. Course I'd be willing to lend them a hand with the parade, or give my advice about the show, but . . . "

"Ha!" Heywood sneered. "You giving advice!"

They had come to Pickett Street. Marvin, who had to stop at the store to see if there were any orders to deliver, turned off. Eddie went with him, and the others continued across the bridge.

On the floor of the grocery were six large cartons, each heaped with tinned food, and Mr. Pratt was filling a seventh with bottles of ketchup. Marvin lifted one of the cartons a few inches off the floor and groaned.

"Gee, Mr. Pratt," he complained, "these'll bust my basket!"

"Not if you don't put them in it." Mr. Pratt seemed to be a little excited. "That's all one order. Biggest I've had since the firemen's convention."

"Where do I have to take them?" Marvin asked. He noted with dismay that Eddie was edging toward the door.

"Man's comin' back for them with a pickup truck." Mr. Pratt studied his empty shelves. "Better break open some more cartons of ketchup and beans, Marvin. Maybe Eddie will give you a hand."

The boys went into the back room and began to shift the stacks of supplies. Ten minutes later, after they had finally located the ketchup, Mr. Pratt called: "The gentleman's here, boys! Hop to it!"

The customer leaning against the counter was the sad-faced man who had been working on the barge. He gloomily gazed at Marvin and Eddie as though he'd never seen them before. Then he jerked his thumb toward the small truck outside.

The boys staggered out the door with one of the cartons and shoved it into the truck beside a stack of oak floorboards. The second carton seemed heavier, and the third and fourth were heavier still.

"You'd think he'd help," Eddie grumbled as they heaved the fifth carton beside the others. "What's he want with all this stuff, anyway? Is he going to Afghanistan to hunt dodos for the next six years?"

Marvin stopped to wipe his forehead. "I wonder who he is . . . and that other guy with the broken nose? They don't look like regular summer folks. More like crooks escaped from a movie. When we left the boat-

yard old Flat-nose leered at us just like that ugly-pussed gangster in——"

A faint, jingling sound interrupted, and both boys wheeled around. Sad-face was standing close behind them, swinging the truck keys. He regarded the boys without expression.

"I don't like to hear talk like that about my friend and me," he said in a low flat voice. "Somethin' unhealthy could happen to kids whose mouths get too big for their brains. Now bring those other cases out."

Marvin and Eddie hurried in for another carton.

Mr. Pratt followed them out with the last one. He placed it on the front seat and let out his breath.

"There you are, sir." He beamed. "That'll keep you in vittles for quite a spell. Goin' on a long campin' trip, are you?"

The man climbed to the seat and started the motor.

"Yeah." He glared meaningly at the boys. "A long campin' trip." He stepped on the gas, and the truck rattled up River Street in the direction of the boatyard.

Marvin scowled after the truck. "And he's going in *our* boat," he muttered. He turned to follow Mr. Pratt into the store. "Come on, Eddie. If you'll help me with the shelves I'll go bug hunting with you."

Some time later Marvin and Eddie, armed with nets, worked their way along the bank of Kinnecong Creek. They were below the playhouse where the creek broadened into its outlet at the river. On their side of the stream three or four sycamores grew from a thicket of weeds and underbrush. On the opposite side a high stone wall rose directly from the water to the back yards of the houses on lower Pickett Street. A stone stairway broke the wall at one place, ending at a long floating dock.

The dock belonged to a man who never used it, and he had offered its use to Marvin and Eddie for any craft they'd care to moor there.

It was exactly the right size for the *Spider Queen,* Marvin thought. How wonderful it would be to see the blue canalboat tied up there now, pulling gently at her hempen hawsers, waiting for her crew of seven to run her into the wide current of the river!

As the two boys regarded the dock with feelings of near anguish, a small butterfly that looked like a scrap of brown wrapping paper fluttered over it. The butterfly started across the creek and the bug hunters' nets went up.

"It's an anglewing," declared Eddie.

"It's a fritillary," corrected Marvin. "It doesn't have any angles."

"I'm not so sure. . . . "

The insect came within a yard of the bank. Then, as though it sensed the purpose of the two raised nets, it turned upstream and disappeared over the millpond. Reluctantly the boys lowered their nets and started down to the river.

"We'll never know now," Marvin said. "There are lots of those brown things that look alike when they're flying. Could have been an admiral or a painted lady. . . ." He stopped to listen to a low throbbing sound that came from downriver. "Hey! Maybe that's the *Spider Queen*!"

They pushed rapidly through the weeds and came out on the open riverbank. Not far away, the barge with two men in its stern was chugging placidly out of

Old Cappy's boatyard. Though it was perhaps the most ancient vessel on the river—and certainly the least streamlined—it rode the inshore current with an air of heavy dignity and calm assurance. No shore was too distant or mysterious for its bow to touch. She was truly a queen—the queen of the river.

Marvin and Eddie sighed. They would someday own a boat, but it wouldn't be the same as this proud sky-blue craft. No combination of hull, motor or sail could ever take its place.

Its throttle now opened to full-speed, the barge swung into the fast midstream current. It steered a straight course toward the bend in the river—the bend that concealed the rocky wooded shores of Locust Island.

"G-golly!" Eddie sighed. "There she goes forever."

"On 'a long campin' trip,' " muttered Marvin.

Eddie snorted. "Camping trip, my foot! The best camping places are *up* the river, not down. And two men couldn't eat all the stuff they took."

"Maybe they're going downriver to pick up a party," suggested Marvin. "Then they'll come back."

"Could be. But even upriver there are lots of towns. Anybody with sense wouldn't bother to lug around a ton of canned stuff unless . . . unless . . . "

"Unless what?"

"Unless," Eddie went on, "they were crooks or escaped convicts planning a hideout. And from the way old Sad-face acted I'd say sure enough he's a crook."

As Marvin gazed at the barge, now small in the distance, the pictures on the post-office bulletin board flashed through his mind.

"Neither one of those men was Smitsy-wicks," he said.

"No," Eddie confirmed. "Those pictures don't fit these two. But that doesn't mean anything, because it's only crooks who commit crimes against the Post Office Department that get their faces on bulletin boards."

Marvin nodded. "Say!" he exclaimed suddenly. "That super-market robbery the other night, and the big jewelry-store holdup in Trenton last month!"

"Yeah!" Eddie rubbed the back of his head while he soberly pondered the river bend. "Locust Island's pretty big," he mused. "My dad says it's about the wildest and rockiest place for a hundred miles around. Hardly anybody ever goes there, and so . . . "

The boys exchanged knowing glances. But just then the brown butterfly danced between them, and they were off into the underbrush with nets waving.

Chapter 8

Rehearsal

MRS. PIPER caught Marvin, Eddie and Heywood the next afternoon as they were crossing the mill-pond bridge. Everything was now organized, she told them. She recited her news of the preparations so fast that the boys could almost feel the words bouncing off their ears.

But they concentrated when she mentioned the clean-up project. To their great relief, she said that the clean-up crews were already formed—the work had been assigned to their schoolmates. Besides this, progress was being made with the remaining details of the celebration: posters were printed and ready for the store windows, the parade route was decided and the show was being written.

"That's swell," Marvin said when she had finished. "We'll come to see everything."

Mrs. Piper smiled at him. "You'll not come to *see* the show—you'll be *in* it."

"Me?" asked Marvin, surprised.

"All of you boys who cleaned up the mill grounds so splendidly. There will be others in it too, of course."

"But . . . but we've never acted before," Eddie protested.

"That won't matter," Mrs. Piper said. "It's going to be a sort of pageant, and there won't be a great deal of acting. At first we were going to ask grownups to take the parts. But we decided that since the early history of Shalerville is the priceless heritage of the younger generation, it would be more appropriate for the school children to be the actors. Now, what do you think of it?"

Nobody had an answer. She went on: "It will be very exciting. Mr. Ziggley is writing it. He's using Obadiah Shaler's old journal for material, though he'll change it some to fit the occasion."

"Will there be Redcoats and Continentals in it?" Heywood asked.

"Oh, yes, indeed! And George Washington too!"

"Dressed up in uniforms?" asked Marvin.

"Yes, you will have uniforms from a theater supply

company. They may be too large, but we can fix that with safety pins. Does it appeal to you?"

"Gee!" cried Marvin. "I . . . I think it's keen!"

"Me, too!" echoed Heywood with enthusiasm. He was already picturing himself lying in ambush with a steady rifle aimed at the road.

Mrs. Piper, pleased with their evident interest, went happily on her way.

In the days that followed, the sidewalks were studded with boxes, baskets and barrels of rubbish. Squads of boys emptied the containers into large trucks which slowly rolled along the streets. Small scatterings of junk on the banks of the creek were attacked, ragged stands of weeds along the towpath and in vacant lots were cut, and old posters were removed from telephone poles. People trimmed their hedges, weeded their gardens and painted their porches. The fire engine was polished and the public cannon given a fresh coat of black paint. A widespread but unsuccessful search was even made for the missing cannon ball.

During this activity the seven boys strolled about the streets to offer encouragement wherever they thought it was needed. Marvin, however, was able to devote only his afternoons to this pleasant occupation, his mornings being spent at the grocery.

It was while he was in the back room removing the tissue wrappers from a crate of grapefruit that he heard Mrs. Piper come into the store and start to talk to Mr. Pratt. Marvin paid little attention to the conversation until he heard her mention the parade. He stopped rattling the grapefruit wrappers and listened.

"We'll need at least two dozen of each of those," she was saying, "and see if you can get us a few stalks of corn."

"Stalks?" asked Mr. Pratt.

"I think the stalks will look better on the float than just ears. It's going to be named 'Abundance,' and the ladies want it to be the most splendid float in the parade."

"Of course, of course, Mrs. Piper," replied Mr. Pratt. "I'll see that you have the biggest of everything. Now, was there anything else?"

"Oh, yes. We decided to spell out the name of our club with carrots. They should look delightful against a magenta background, don't you think?"

Mr. Pratt cleared his throat. "Hmm, yes. My favorite colors. How many carrots do you figure on?"

At this point Marvin heard his name called from across the millpond. He looked out the window and saw Eddie standing on the opposite shore near the theater.

"Hi, Eddie!" he shouted. "What's up?"

"You're George Washington," Eddie shouted back.

"You're the Queen of Mongolia," yelled Marvin.

"I'm not kidding," yelled Eddie. "You're the father of his country in the play."

Marvin was speechless for a minute. Then he hollered, "How do you know?"

"Mrs. Piper's been handing out parts all over town. Yours is at home. She says there'll be a rehearsal this afternoon."

"She's here now," Marvin yelled, "buying cornstalks and carrots . . . and magentas—whatever they are."

"Stop that yelling, Marvin," called Mr. Pratt from the store.

"See you later, Eddie." Marvin turned back to the grapefruit. He wondered how he would look in a white wig and a general's uniform, and whether or not they would let him have a horse.

Marvin and Eddie arrived at the playhouse grounds much too early for the rehearsal. No one else was there, so they sprawled out on the grass and studied their typewritten scripts.

They read for a long time, silently absorbed in the exciting tale of Shalerville's part in the Revolution. The play was in one act, to be performed against a painted backdrop representing the office of the Shaler Mill.

The story itself was hard to follow. There were many characters, and they were always being interrupted by runners with messages and by groups of millers and barefoot Continentals crossing the stage. Yet the story did move along in a beclouded way. It was the story of Obadiah Shaler's invaluable assistance to the harassed General Washington, and of how the citizens of Shaler Village helped win the war for the Continental Congress.

Best of all was the grand finale. At the close of the act soldiers and villagers were to march off the stage, through a theater exit, and down to the shore of the Delaware River. The audience would follow. Then Washington and some of the soldiers would get in a boat and push off for the "Battle of Trenton."

"Boy, that's a keen ending!" Eddie remarked. "I wonder whose boat they'll use."

"Who knows?" Marvin shrugged, painfully remembering his last view of the barge. He turned over the pages of his script. "Who do you play?"

"I'm Corporal Bluegate of the First Pennsylvania Rifles. I keep running around with messages."

Marvin leafed some more through the script. "Page ten—you 'burst into the mill office with labored breathing.' . . . What do you say we act out the scene to see how it goes?"

"Okay. You're Washington and I'm Bluegate. You sit on that rock over there and I'll burst up to you."

Marvin sat on the rock. Eddie ran over to him, breathing as loud as he could.

" 'What is the meaning of this intrusion?' " Marvin read. " 'Do you not see that I am busily poring over a map which shows the breastworks and emplacements

of the British who are joined with the Hessians on the other side of the river near Trenton? Well, speak up, Corp Bluegate.' "

" 'Begging your pardon, sir,' " read Eddie, " 'but I bring in . . . incalcu . . . lably important information from my commander, Lieutenant James Monroe, who has quarters at the neighboring village of Solebury in a mill—not so large as this one, I may say, sir. Looks around.' "

Marvin made a face. "You aren't supposed to say 'looks around.' That's just directions for what you *do*."

"Oh, yeah. I see. Well, go ahead—you're next."

" 'Out with it, Corp.' "

"That's 'corporal,' stupid."

" 'Out with it, Corporal.' "

" 'Lieutenant Monroe sends his greetings and wishes to inform you that he has captured three men of the British regulars who crossed the river on a raft to reconnoiter our positions.' "

" 'Hmm, hmm.' . . . That means I'm thinking," Marvin explained.

" 'They are at this very minute being sent here under heavy guard and will be here any minute.' "

" 'Good. You must be sore and fatigued, Corporal Bluegate. Go to my host, Obadiah Shaler, who was the first miller in this county. He will give you a billet.' "

"I exit," said Eddie, "and you pore over your map. I guess that means you have coffee or something."

"I tasted coffee once," Marvin said. "I spit it back though."

"Yeah. I don't like it either. Maybe Mr. Ziggley'd change it to pop if you asked him. No reason why you couldn't pour pop on the map."

"Guess not," said Marvin. "But it sounds like a goofy thing to do."

"The map could have been made with a secret invisible ink," Eddie pointed out. "And there'd be a chemical in the coffee that would make it visible. The FBI does stuff like that."

Heywood and Gilbert arrived just then with their scripts and flopped to the grass.

"Who are you guys?" Eddie asked.

"I'm Obadiah Shaler," Heywood said, "and Gilbert's the regiment commander named De Fermoy."

"I'm quartered at Shaler's Mill," said Gilbert. "They quarter officers and billet soldiers," he explained. "I hear that you're George Washington," he said to Marvin.

"Yes," admitted Marvin modestly.

"Boy, you've got to act real important!" Heywood observed. "You've got to carry yourself erect, like it says in the directions."

Other players were arriving. School children of many ages and sizes chased one another about the grounds as though the rehearsal were another picnic. They threw stones into the millpond, climbed into a willow tree, wrestled in the grass, and a lot of girls chattered on the playhouse steps.

Mrs. Piper and Mr. Ziggley drove up the driveway.

"Everyone inside!" called Mrs. Piper when she got out of the car.

She and Mr. Ziggley led the straggling children through the double door of the playhouse and down the aisle to the front of the auditorium. The stage was set up like a modern apartment in New York—a scene for the play that the summer-theater actors were giving that week. A woman was trying to straighten the slats in a Venetian blind, and someone was hammering behind the painted canvas wall.

"Stop the hammering!" Mr. Ziggley shouted.

When the hammering stopped, Mrs. Piper began to explain the pageant. "It will be given next Friday evening," she said. "So we'll have to work hard. The seventh-grade girls will be the chorus. They open the play with a song about the building of Shaler's Mill. While they're singing, millworkers cross the stage with sacks of flour on their shoulders. They will softly recite: 'We, the faithful millers are; for daily bread we grind the flour.' " She glanced at Mr. Ziggley. "Is that right?"

The mayor nodded.

Mrs. Piper gave some more directions, and the first rehearsal of *O Shalerville* began. The actors read their parts, and the chorus stumbled along with frequent interruptions of song. Mrs. Piper and Mr. Ziggley sat in the first row of seats and kept it all going.

During a scene in which Marvin was alone on the stage, Mr. Ziggley waved his glasses and asked him to stop.

"Washington," he said, "you are sick at heart. The Continental Congress has delayed getting shoes to your suffering men. All is black—you are ready to retreat. Now, try this scene again and make it as sad as you can."

Marvin drooped his head as far as it would go without tipping him over. Then he read from his script in a loud shaky voice: " 'O my dire suffering soldiers! Alas! Would they had footwear for their freezing feet.' "

"Now pound," said Mr. Ziggley.

Marvin hurried over to the wall and began to pound his fists on it. " 'It is a pity!' " he shouted. " 'We shall have to retreat again! Perhaps . . . perhaps to Valley Forge!' "

A stagehand with a hammer pulled up the Venetian blind and climbed through the window of the New York apartment.

He grabbed Marvin's swinging arm. "You want to bust a hole through the canvas?" he yelled.

"I guess not," said Marvin.

The man dropped Marvin's arm and scowled at Mr. Ziggley. "This stage-set's got to last the rest of the week, and if he pounds it full of holes . . . "

Mr. Ziggley loosened his necktie. "All right," he said. "Pound on the desk, Washington."

The man left. But before Marvin could start pounding on the desk, Heywood came running onto the stage, announcing to Washington: " 'The citizens of Shaler Village are giving up their very own shoes for the cause of freedom. Even little children are tearing theirs from their feet, and——' "

"Children's shoes wouldn't fit the soldiers," Mrs. Piper objected to Mr. Ziggley. "Can't we leave that out?"

"The children must make a sacrifice for freedom, too," Mr. Ziggley argued. "Their shoes could be returned when it's later discovered they won't fit."

"But they should have sense enough to know——"

"Mrs. Piper, have you ever experienced the inspired fever of patriotism?" asked Mr. Ziggley. "They haven't time to think of things like that. The children give their own poor footgear with unselfish devotion."

"I still don't think——" began Mrs. Piper.

"It will not be noticed," said Mr. Ziggley.

"But I'm sure it *will* be noticed," returned Mrs. Piper.

While this argument was going on, villagers filed across the stage, dropping their shoes in a pile. Emery came in and saluted. Then the hammering began again.

"Stop that hammering!" cried Mr. Ziggley, rising from his seat.

"When do I stop saluting, Mr. Ziggley?" Emery asked.

Mr. Ziggley didn't hear him, for Corporal Bluegate had just raced up to Washington, breathing loudly. Before Bluegate could say anything, the stagehand stuck his head through the apartment window.

"Mr. Ziggley," he said, "if I can't hammer down those flat-supports, the regular show won't go on tonight."

"Can I stop saluting now?" asked Emery.

"When the last shoe falls," said Mr. Ziggley in a tense voice.

"If I can't hammer——" said the stagehand.

Mr. Ziggley's face reddened and he started for the door. "All *right*!" he yelled. "Go and hammer!"

The door slammed behind him, and for a minute there was complete silence. Finally the stagehand crawled back through the window. As his hammering shook the walls the villagers scrambled for their shoes, and Mrs. Piper loudly instructed everyone about future rehearsals to be held at the high-school auditorium.

Outside at last, Marvin, Eddie, Heywood and Emery walked together along the gravel drive.

"Boy," Eddie said, "that's going to be some show!"

"Aw, the first part's not much good!" said Heywood. "Just singing and talking and that shoe business. Wait'll we act out the last part. That's when the real action comes—Redcoats and shooting and a slam-bang fight!"

"That's the scene where I beat a drum," said Emery.

"Uh-huh," grunted Heywood. "Say," he went on, "let's go and see if Cappy's got any new vessels. Even if he hasn't I'm about ready to settle for a shad boat, stink or no stink."

"Not me," objected Marvin. "The *Spider Queen* is the only boat *I* want. Maybe we can still get her."

"Aw, why don't you forget it!" put in Heywood. "We'll never see the thing again. Those two crooks——"

"Why don't we report them to the constable?" asked Emery.

Marvin shot a look at Eddie. He remembered the unmistakable warning Sad-face had given them at the store, and he didn't want to start something he couldn't finish.

"We're not sure they're criminals," he said. "Besides, if the constable went down to the island, Sad-face and Flat-nose would probably hit the river. And then, for sure, we'd never see the barge again."

"You got a plan?" asked Heywood.

"No, but I was thinking that if we could get to the island without them seeing us, we might be able to find out something—if they're on the island at all. If we could prove they're really crooks they'd go to jail, and somehow we might be able to get the *Spider Queen.*"

Emery gave his brother a bitter look. "If you go making up a plan," he warned, "it had better be different from that last one. I'd join up with the crooks before you could get me into another dress!"

Chapter 9

The Parade

MAYOR ZIGGLEY had declared the day of the grand celebration a half holiday. Promptly on the shrill note of the bag factory's noon whistle, Shalerville's stores and shops closed.

Shortly afterward the sidewalks became cluttered with people hurrying to the fire station. There were soldiers in freshly pressed uniforms, bandsmen with their instruments, children on decorated bicycles, Boy Scouts, Girl Scouts, and just ordinary people who didn't want to miss any of the big parade.

Marvin and Eddie, in new overalls, red bandannas and straw hats, wheeled along the street toward Mrs. Piper's house. They were to be "farmers" on the Ladies Club float. They passed the center of town, wobbled through the gathering crowd, and turned into the Piper driveway. Several women were there, busily adding last-minute touches to the "Abundance" float.

It was a large wide hay wagon from a near-by farm. Draped from front to rear with colored crepe paper and stacked high with fruits, vegetables and bunches of flowers, it was the fanciest thing the boys had ever seen. On each side was the name of the club spelled in carrots on a bright-red background. Near the front of the platform was a leaf-covered throne. It faced backward and was under an arch on which "Abundance" was spelled in small yellow apples.

Marvin and Eddie stared at it with wonder.

"How do you like it?" asked Mrs. Piper, coming up.

"Wow," said Eddie quietly.

"Prettiest thing I ever saw!" said Marvin.

"Thank you." Mrs. Piper beamed. "The wagon gives it such a nice old-fashioned touch, don't you think?"

"Sure does," Marvin said.

The owner of the hay wagon came up the drive with a team of big white farm horses. He whoa-ed them to a stop, then blotted his forehead with a red handkerchief.

"The day's a sizzler," he remarked. "Hotter 'n a bushel o' baked potatoes." He nodded toward the float. "Won't them-there posies droop?"

One of the ladies patted Marvin and Eddie on their straw hats. "We have two little gardeners—" she giggled—"to sprinkle them during the parade with two little sprinkling cans."

As the boys' faces turned red, Mr. Thorpe—the farmer—winked at them. "Take it easy, fellas, and don't flood the float." He backed the team to the wagon and began the task of hitching.

A plump high-school girl came out of the house. Her white dress was so long that it dragged on the porch steps. A huge bunch of sweet peas was on top of her head.

The ladies fluttered about her and squealed. "Oh, Bernice, you're simply *darling*!" cried one. And another said, "A vision, simply a vision!"

"Just the *picture* of abundance!" said Mrs. Piper. "How do you like our queen, Mr. Thorpe?"

Mr. Thorpe couldn't think of anything to say, and Mrs. Piper went to assist the others with the seating of Bernice on the throne. They spent a lot of time arranging the folds of her dress and trying the sweet peas in different places on her head.

At last, when the queen was fixed, Mrs. Piper beckoned to Marvin and Eddie. Then she began to hunt through the vegetables, as though she had lost something.

"Aha!" she said. "Here they are! The cleared spaces for your feet—two for each of you."

The boys climbed onto the wagon and gingerly planted their feet in the spaces.

Marvin looked worried. "What do we do if the wagon jerks?"

"Clear a place real quick to sit in if it does." Mr. Thorpe grinned.

"Yes," said Mrs. Piper. "Now, there is a keg of water behind the potatoes, boys. Fill your sprinkling cans whenever they're empty. Keep the flowers nice and fresh . . . and the rhubarb leaves and the lettuce."

Just then the sound of drums came from the direction of the fire station.

Mrs. Piper looked at her wrist watch. "The parade is forming," she said excitedly. "We should leave. Are you ready, Bernice?"

"Yes."

"Boys?"

"Yes."

"Mr. Thorpe?"

"Yes, ma'am."

"Then tell the horses to go, Mr. Thorpe."

The street in front of the fire station was a riot of noise, movement and color. People from all over the county jammed the sidewalks and mingled with the units of the parade as it assembled. Uniforms and brass musical instruments flashed in the sun. Orders rang out, drums thumped experimentally, clarinets and trumpets squawked and played trills. Gaudy floats jockeyed into their positions.

Suddenly the sharp note of a whistle shrilled over

the hubbub. A moment later a shimmering crash of cymbals and a series of blue-smoke backfires from the constable's glistening motorcycle got the parade under way. Behind the stiffly erect, stern-faced constable came the color-bearers with gold-fringed flags. Next came an open car with Mr. Ziggley, Mr. Shaler and Mrs. Van Trant in the back seat. Then came the band with Emery supporting the bass drum and blinking at each throbbing onslaught of thunder in the "Thunder and Cavalry March."

Behind the band were the war veterans, then the fire engine—with the Bakerstown hook-and-ladder truck as its guest—then a float called "Our Early Days," the Boy Scouts, the "Abundance" float, the Girl Scouts, a float decorated with empty cement bags from the bag company, and the Post 400 drum-and-bugle corps with its thumping and blasting. There were more floats, followed by a line of cars, motorcycles and bicycles, all tangled with yards of crepe-paper streamers.

Tremendous cheers arose from the side lines. Canes with Shalerville pennants waved wildly. Children bobbed gas-filled balloons sold by hustling venders. People waved from windows and rooftops. It was the biggest, noisiest parade ever to walk the narrow streets of Shalerville.

It proceeded from the fire station to the center of town. From there it swung to the right on Bridge Street, with the Shaler Mill as its destination.

On the bumping "Abundance," Marvin and Eddie were having a little trouble keeping on their feet. But they proudly kept their heads up, and lowered their eyes only occasionally to examine the flowers and the vegetables.

As they started up the short grade to the bridge, Marvin spoke from the corner of his mouth: "Lettuce drooping. Your side."

Without noticeably looking at the lettuce, Eddie gave it a fast sprinkle. "Much obliged. Daisies, your side."

Marvin started to sprinkle them, but at that moment Mr. Thorpe hollered "Whoa!" The "Abundance" stopped, and the dreaded jerk came with a suddenness that pitched both boys onto their faces—Marvin's in the rhubarb and Eddie's in the freshly sprinkled lettuce.

Water from the keg behind the potatoes slopped in a wave toward the throne. Gasping in horror, the queen grabbed at her dress. But she was too late. Her dripping skirt was like a soaked rag pulled out of a laundry tub.

Mr. Thorpe peered around the cornstalks from the driver's seat. "Freight train settin' on the crossin' up ahead," he explained.

Just then a crash was heard farther back in the parade.

Marvin and Eddie, on hands and knees, looked at each other.

"Sounded like that gift-shop float with all the Mexican pottery," said Marvin.

"Yeah," murmured Eddie. "Golly, I'd like to go back and see it."

"We've got our duty," said Marvin. "Those old daisies . . . " He refilled his can from the water remaining in the keg and sprinkled the daisies again.

Pretty soon a whistle blew at the head of the parade. The band stopped. There was silence for a moment. Then the constable's motorcycle roared, the whistle blew again, and the band vibrated with the solemn chords of "Shalerville, Dear Shalerville."

Eddie looked ahead through the cornstalks. "Hey, they're doubling back on us!" he exclaimed. "I guess they couldn't get the train to move."

"Engineer's probably gone for lunch," said Marvin, sprinkling some turnips.

"How are they going to get past us, I'd like to know?" Eddie said. "We're right in the middle of this skinny little bridge."

Marvin now looked for himself. The constable was already alongside the Boy Scouts and slowing down for the "Abundance." Marching in the smoke of his exhaust were the color-bearers, followed by Mr. Ziggley's car, the band and the veterans. The fire engines were maneuvering a turn at the blocked railroad crossing.

When the constable stopped at the hay wagon, Mr.

Thorpe scowled down on him. "How am I gonna get this wagon ahead with you and ever'thing else on the bridge?" he asked.

"You'll have to back up," ordered the constable.

"With all them little Girl Scouts behind us fallin' under the wagon?"

"They'll have to back up, too."

"Into the cement-bag float?"

"*It* will have to . . ." The constable shut his mouth tightly and got off his motorcycle. "Let me crawl under your overhang," he growled.

He propped up his motorcycle and disappeared under the wagon. He soon reappeared and trotted down the line of the parade, speaking to squad leaders and float drivers.

After a long time the people and things behind the hay wagon began to retreat. When the Girl Scouts finally moved away, Mr. Thorpe stood on the edge of the wagon with the reins in his hands. He looked back, squinting at the extremely narrow space between the float and the two concrete bridge rails.

"This has got to be good and straight," he said. "I'll go slow, and you boys watch them rear corners. . . . Back up, Mabel, Gussie! Easy . . . easy . . . *easy!*"

But the horses, bothered by the band, were in a hurry.

"Whoa!" shouted Marvin, Eddie and Mr. Thorpe together as the float spun at an angle across the bridge.

Two of its corners splintered against the railings. The whole wagon bulged upward in the middle, with water sloshing and vegetables rolling off the sides. The queen disappeared under a mass of potatoes and toppling cornstalks.

Mr. Thorpe yelled something good and loud at the band and jumped down to pull the rearing horses back to the pavement.

Marvin slowly raised himself from the rhubarb. "Eddie! You still here?" he called.

"I'm under the throne," answered a muffled voice.

"Well, come out and sprinkle your lettuce. You'll catch it from Mrs. Piper!"

After a while things began to improve. The band stopped playing, the horses quit jumping, Eddie dug himself into the open, and the constable returned.

The officer of the law stumbled over the wreckage and went to talk to Mr. Thorpe.

"Can you clear the bridge?" he asked in a peeved tone.

"Backward?" asked Mr. Thorpe.

The constable stuck out his lower lip. "Forward," he said.

"Over the band?"

"The band will back up."

"Into the soldiers?"

The constable glared at Mr. Thorpe for a few seconds. Suddenly he began to laugh softly. Then he turned on his heel, crawled back over the vegetables, stalked past the Girl Scouts, the cement-bag float, the Post 400, and vanished in the crowd.

It was fifteen minutes before the freight train yanked itself into life. With echoing clanks along its length it gathered speed. The caboose finally passed and the crossing gates went up.

Mr. Ziggley got out of his car and came over to the "Abundance."

"The front part of the parade will proceed to the mill as planned," he said to Mr. Thorpe, who was still holding the horses. "And the part that's behind you will back down to River Street. It will then go frontward to the mill by way of Pickett Street. We've been frittering our time." He looked critically at the hay wagon. "You will remain here, I suppose?"

"Till the band and them tin horns is out of earshot," said Mr. Thorpe. "Maybe a sight longer."

A great deal of backing, turning, drum beating, whistle blowing, and shouting followed. Someone wheeled the constable's motorcycle toward the freight station. The band crossed the tracks and began "Thunder and Cavalry." Soon the front section of the parade was a block away and turning into Jupiter Street. The rear section had backed down to River Street and was getting started, frontward, to the blare of its bugles.

Mrs. Piper and two ladies pushed through the crowd of wide-eyed children who had gathered around the "Abundance." There were lines of tragedy on the club president's face.

"Oh dear, Mr. Thorpe!" she cried. "Just look at our float!"

"Our beautiful float," wailed one of the ladies.

"Mabel and Gussie'll get it unstuck," said Mr. Thorpe in a calm voice. "You ladies just drive on up t' the mill and listen to the speeches. And don't go frettin' yourselves 'bout this-here mishap."

Mrs. Piper suddenly saw a stockinged foot protruding from the potatoes. She screamed. "Bernice! Oh, heavens! Somebody get her out!"

The boys and Mr. Thorpe dug into the potatoes for the queen and stood her up. She swayed a little and began to pull the sweet peas out of her hair.

To hide a grin, Marvin turned toward River Street,

where the last stragglers of the parade were disappearing behind the drugstore. Abruptly he straightened. The flat-nosed man, carrying two large oilcans, was going down to a dock near the Bakerstown bridge!

Marvin grabbed Eddie's arm and pointed. "He's got a boat down there," he whispered. "Maybe it's the *Spider Queen*. . . . Let's trail him!"

"How?" Eddie whispered back.

"On our bikes—down River Road. We could keep an eye on him through the trees."

"Okay. But what about this stuff?" Eddie indicated the mess around them. "Maybe we ought to——"

As though in answer Mrs. Piper looked up at the boys. "Thank you so much," she said. "You did a splendid job—just splendid. I'm sure you don't want to miss the speeches. So, if you care to, you may go."

"You're sure—?" began Marvin.

"There are enough willing hands." She smiled at the children around the wagon. "And I know Mr. Thorpe can manage the horses."

"Yep," said Mr. Thorpe. "One good yank and we'll be loose. You two sprinklers run along."

Before he had finished his sentence the boys were racing toward the Bakerstown bridge. When they reached a place where they could look down at the dock, they halted. Flat-nose was just starting the engine of a small motorboat.

"Come on!" Marvin led the way around the corner and up the street to Mrs. Piper's house. The moment they leaped on their bikes they heard the motorboat leave the dock.

They had never pedaled so fast. They whizzed through the empty town, over the millpond bridge, past Pickett Street and the end of the parade, then the boatyard and the canal. In three minutes they were out of Shalerville.

They slowed down to listen. The *putt-putt* of the outboard came from behind them, so they rode on more leisurely to a place beyond the bag factory where they could get a clear view of the river. They waited until they saw the boat. Then they continued along the road, keeping abreast and catching occasional glimpses of it through the trees. Flat-nose appeared in the distance to be no more menacing than an innocent vacationist or fisherman.

"I'll bet half of my water bugs that he stops at Locust Island," Marvin said.

"I sure hope he does," returned Eddie. "I'm not in the mood to pump this bike to Trenton or Philadelphia. Besides, I've got to save my strength for the pageant tonight."

As the boat neared the island's tip they were elated to hear the outboard cut to half speed. Wheeling fast, they reached a clearing by the road. They dropped their bicycles and pushed through some weeds just in time to see Flat-nose swing the boat out of sight between the island and the opposite shore of the river.

"Wouldn't you know!" moaned Eddie.

"That's a good sign," Marvin pointed out. "It's suspicious. This shore of the river has a road along it, but the other one's just woods and a high rock bank. If he puts in at the island on that side, nobody'd see him. Listen!" He held up his hand.

The *putt-putting,* which they heard faintly through the island's trees, slowed and then stopped. The boys barely breathed. They listened for a minute or two longer, but the boat didn't start again.

At last Marvin relaxed. "We were right," he said with a grin. "And I'll bet *all* of my water bugs that the *Spider Queen* is tied up there."

"Uh-huh. But what can we do about it?"

Marvin studied the thickly wooded island and its rocky shore line. It would be pretty dangerous to land a boat there, he thought. Except, maybe, on the strip of sand among the rocks about fifty yards from the island's tip. Of course the two men probably kept a constant watch. Maybe even this minute . . .

Suddenly an idea made his eyes sparkle. He knew now what he and his well-experienced raiding party could do about it!

He turned for the road. "Come on, Eddie! We've got to round up the gang. We're going to have a secret meeting, and right away quick!"

Chapter 10

O Shalerville

THAT EVENING the two dressing rooms behind the playhouse stage were a clutter of Colonial costumes, soldier uniforms, wooden muskets, powdered wigs, and excited boys and girls.

In the girls' room Mrs. Piper and other members of the Ladies Club busily applied grease paint and powder on upturned faces. They pinned the hems of too-long skirts and fussed with bows and frills. Mrs. Van Trant and Mr. Shaler, in the boys' room, struggled with boots, grease paint, false beards and safety pins.

Mr. Ziggley nervously paced back and forth between the dressing rooms and the stage. Every minute or so he peeked through the curtain at the fast-growing audience, then badgered the players with pleas to hurry.

The girls of the chorus were the first to be ready. Giggling a little, they gathered in a wing of the stage to await the signal to take their places in the orchestra pit. One by one the others left the dressing rooms. They stood in groups, studying their parts and adjusting oversize collars, belts and three-cornered hats. Two or three club ladies puttered at the rude furnishings of the stage. They moved chairs an inch this way or that way, and they brushed imaginary dust from Obadiah's desk and the canvas walls of the set.

At last all was ready. Mrs. Piper led the chorus through the curtain and down to the orchestra pit. Heywood, gray-bearded and dressed in knee breeches, checkered shirt and a flour-sprinkled apron, sat at the desk on the stage. The lights of the packed auditorium went down and the chorus burst into song. The curtain went up.

The millers, carrying sawdust-filled bags, filed onto the stage reciting: "We, the faithful millers are."

Customers and millers came and went. Obadiah stood at his desk and then he sat at it. There were thumpings and rattlings off stage that mimicked the sounds of mill machinery. People knocked at the office door. Messages of the army's approach kept arriving. Then George Washington strode into the spotlight. Cheers from the audience rocked the theater.

Marvin was so surprised by the applause that he forgot his first line. While a hushed audience waited, he stood and thought. He pulled up one of his boots a little higher. Someone coughed.

"Ah, miller Shaler," Mr. Ziggley prompted from the stage wing.

Marvin faced Heywood. "Ah, shiller Shaler," he said hoarsely. "I am weary. My men are sore and hungry. It is patriotic of you to put up with us . . . to put us up. Has my quartermaster made arrangement with you for quarters and billets? Fine. I am glad to hear it."

"Yes, he has," said Heywood.

With alternate scenes of inspiration and despair, the pageant reached the halfway mark. Here the curtain was lowered to indicate a brief passage of time.

Marvin straightened his sword belt and walked off the stage.

The eighth-grade boy who operated the curtain looked at him admiringly. "You acted that swell," he said. "Will there be fighting in the next scene?"

"Sure," said Marvin. "Lots of it. A gang of Redcoats attack the mill. And wait till you see our rifles—they look just like real ones!"

"Wow, that'll be something! You in it?"

"Not at first. I come in later to settle the fight with strategy."

Marvin's eye was attracted to something moving above his head on one of the curtain ropes. It was a large green praying mantis—a wily insect that he would give anything to capture. It clung to the rope with its four back legs and held the other two in a praying position in front of its face. With insolent eyes it stared downward, as though daring Marvin to come and get him.

Out in front the chorus began to sing about darkening horizons.

"When do you pull up the curtain?" Marvin asked the curtain boy.

"When the singers hit a long high note and somebody shoots off a bunch of firecrackers."

"Would you let me pull it up?"

The eighth-grader hesitated, but finally he shrugged and handed Marvin the rope. "Okay. I'm going for a bottle of pop."

Alone at the ropes, Marvin kept an eye on the mantis. It remained motionless, seeming either scornful or ignorant of the threat that waited below.

The high note from the chorus came at last—a

splintering sound that was more like a panther's scream than a musical note. Immediately a number of giant firecrackers exploded backstage.

"Now, mantis!" Marvin grinned. "You're coming down!"

Slowly, slowly, he pulled on the rope, guarding against any accidental jerk that would warn the approaching insect. Now it was only three feet above his hands . . . now two feet . . . one foot . . . six inches.

Suddenly it turned and skittered upward. Marvin gave the rope a terrific pull. It slipped from his hands and whistled on its way to the upper darkness of the stage well.

Down crashed the curtain in a cloud of dust!

The audience let out a shriek that carried across the river. Frightened Redcoats, Continentals, millers and villagers stumbled around in the dust and through the rumpled folds of the curtain. Mr. Ziggley ran across the stage in search of the curtain boy. He saw Marvin and stopped.

"Where'd he go?" he demanded.

Marvin, who had been caught around his chest by a loop of the rope, was spinning a few inches off the floor. Keenly disappointed at the loss of the mantis, he pointed upward.

"He was hanging on the rope the last I saw him," Marvin answered. "With his feet in front of his face, praying-like."

Mr. Ziggley stared into the darkness above. "Oh, my!" He gasped. "Somebody, go for a ladder!"

Marvin stopped revolving. Then he started going around in the other direction.

"Oh, that's all right, Mr. Ziggley," he said. "He's probably flown away by now."

"Flown . . . away?" said Mr. Ziggley quietly. He grabbed Marvin's shoulders to hold him still. "Flown where?"

"Golly, Mr. Ziggley, I don't know. But don't worry about it. I'll find another sometime."

"Another curtain boy?"

"Another mantis."

Mr. Ziggley took a deep breath. "What is a mantis?"

"A big green bug. If I find another I'll show him to you."

Mr. Ziggley sat down on a box and held his head in his hands.

Marvin started to go around again. But Mr. Shaler, coming into the wing, soon untangled him and set him on his feet.

"Can . . . can we fix it?" Marvin asked.

Mr. Shaler shook his head. "It would take all night. And we can't get it off the stage without cutting the ropes. There's only one thing to do." The flicker of a smile crossed his face, then he crawled over the fallen curtain and went to the front of the stage.

"Your attention, please!" he called out. When the

audience was quiet he went on. "The years of the Revolution in Shaler Village were hard years of privation and suffering, but our ancestors triumphed over every obstacle to survival. Because of their struggle, we enjoy today a heritage of which we can be justly proud. It is fitting, therefore, that the directors and the cast of this pageant give evidence to those brave spirits that the quality of perseverance has not vanished, but still lives in the hearts of our citizens. The play will go on, despite this lumpy obstacle which has fallen among us."

He bowed to loud applause and retired.

A second batch of firecrackers exploded as a lieutenant ran onto the stage shouting "The Redcoats are coming!"

Because of the curtain, sprawled like a mountain ridge along the floor, nothing could be seen of the lieutenant but his head and shoulders. He seemed to realize how strange this must look out front, for he climbed to the top of the curtain and repeated: "The Redcoats are coming!" As he jumped down, other heads appeared. Obadiah, some villagers and more soldiers began to run around, while messengers called out messages and the lieutenant barked orders. Someone was passing out something to the others, but what it was the audience could not tell, until one of the soldiers held up a wooden rifle so all could see.

"Here they come!" a miller cried, and the memorable Battle of Shaler's Mill began.

The confusion became louder and more tangled. Heads came and went. They passed and repassed, bobbed up in unexpected places and vanished. More fireworks banged. The beating on a bass drum in the stage wing gradually became wilder. Now and then a piercing cry broke through the din and the head of a stricken soldier would disappear. There was a tinkle of glass and a splintering of wood. Then, as though the cannonade had burst a storage room, a great puff of flour dust rolled across the stage and hung, curling, in the air.

Through the flour came the cloudy figure of George Washington, the commander in chief. He stumbled along the crest of the curtain and stopped halfway out. He waved his sword. He seemed to be talking, though no one heard him. His presence, however, had a miraculous effect. Little by little the battle sounds diminished, and at last there was order and quiet.

The audience sighed gratefully.

The pageant now continued in a more gentle way. Because of the flour-covered heads, it was impossible to tell who any of the actors were. But no one seemed to mind and the show went through to the end. While the chorus sang "The miller will take them o'er the river, the river," the actors marched off the stage. They went through a rear exit, then down to the river where a motorboat—one that Old Cappy rented to fish-

ing parties—lay secured at a small dock. The audience funneled through the exit and broke across the floodlighted ground like a tidal wave, forcing the chorus and the players to huddle closer about the boat.

Marvin got into it and stood with one foot on the front seat. He noted with satisfaction that Mr. Ziggley had remembered to have a number of twenty-five-pound blocks of ice fastened to the sides of the boat with lengths of clothesline. Five Continentals—personally chosen by Marvin—climbed in, and Heywood took his seat by the motor.

"Good citizens of Shaler Village!" Marvin shouted. "It is your unselfish patriotism which inspires me to march against the Hessians at Trenton. I bestow on you my gratitude, everlasting and internal."

One of the villagers handed him a flag. The chorus

began the strains of "America," and Heywood started the engine.

As the boat moved into the dark river the crowd sent up a thunderous cheer. Hats, hands and handkerchiefs waved while the chorus sang as loudly as it could. The boys on the boat forgot they were actors. They thrilled to the cheer. They felt they had slipped back in Time, that this was Christmas of 1776 with its anxiety and its hope. They were not boys, but men—men charged with a mission to free America from foreign rule.

The ice gently clunked against the sides of the boat, and Marvin, shivering, pulled up the big collar of his coat. He wondered if he could surprise the Hessians. He had a good chance. They certainly would not be expecting an attack on a night as cold as this, with dangerous ice in the Delaware. . . . He would like to take Trenton without a fight if he could. His men must be fast and quiet. . . .

In midstream Heywood turned the boat downriver. It fairly raced along in the current.

"Why are we going this way?" asked Gilbert. "I thought we were supposed to turn around and go back."

Heywood looked at him seriously. "This isn't a pageant any more," he said. "There's going to be a *real* battle."

Gilbert's mouth fell open, and he glanced toward the

fast-disappearing shore they had left. Faint strains of "America" drifted across the water.

"Wh-what battle?" he asked.

"Tell him," Marvin said. "We couldn't find him before the show. So he's the only one who doesn't know where we're going, and he's got to be ready for the attack."

Chapter 11

The Battle of Locust Island

As THEY approached Locust Island, Heywood cut the motor. The unlighted boat slipped silently onward under a clouded half-moon. Each member of the raiding party edged forward. Nerves were tense, heartbeats quickened and eyes strained to pierce the gloom ahead. No one thought to look back to where a searchlight from the distant playhouse frantically swept across the water.

Marvin, crouched in the bow, raised an arm. Heywood swung the boat to the left and brought it to the shadowed rocks of the island shore. At another signal the boat veered sharply. With a little grating sound it ran onto the sand of the narrow beach that Marvin had seen from the road that afternoon.

One by one the blue-uniformed Continentals leaped ashore. While Marvin and Eddie studied the beach and the growth about it, the others busily untied ropes from the boatrail and dragged the blocks of ice to the sand. This went quickly, and in a minute all heads were together for final instructions.

"We're going to split up," Marvin whispered. "Bluegate and I are going up a trail we discovered that leads into the woods from the beach. We'll see if we can locate the hideout. The rest of you go around the tip of the island, as planned. Heywood, Tom and Emery have flashlights. They'll use them only if it's desperately necessary. Make it double quick and come back here to report. We won't have much time before searching parties find our boat and come looking for us. Fast now!"

As four Continentals and the bearded miller loped off into the dark, Washington and Bluegate pushed up the trail toward the middle of the island. It was a difficult path—steep, rocky and snarled with briers and locust saplings. Evidently it was seldom used, if ever.

A branch pushed Eddie's three-cornered hat over his face. "Doggone——" he began. But instantly he found Marvin's hand on his mouth.

"My orders, Corporal Bluegate," whispered Marvin, "are for dead silence, sir."

"Aye, aye," whispered Eddie, straightening his hat.

They halted at the top of the path for breath.

"See anything?" Eddie asked. "I mean, anything, *sir.*"

"Not a thing, Corp. We'll push on."

They pushed on, sparingly using the flashlights they had hidden in the boat before the show. They came abruptly upon a great jumble of rocks, some of which seemed to be as big as houses. In the half-light it looked like something on the moon, and for a minute neither of the boys felt very much like a soldier.

A pale luna moth drifted over the rocks. It was going toward a light!

Both boys saw the faint gleam at once.

"It . . . it comes right out of the rocks," Eddie stammered.

"Yeah. Must be a cave. A cave'd make a super hideout!" Marvin gingerly started over the rocks. "Come on, Bluegate. We'll reconnoiter the situation."

They silently stalked the light and soon discovered they were right. The glow came from a well-camouflaged cave among some of the largest of the rocks. Keeping in the shadows, they approached the cave from one side. They halted a few feet from its entrance. A man came out and they quickly ducked behind a boulder. The man was Sad-face.

"It ain't going to get any darker," he said, looking at the sky.

"Okay, okay!" came an annoyed reply from the cave. "We're gettin' ready, ain't we? But I still say we got a nice little place here, and we're saps to let a couple of kids run us out."

At that moment the big moth, with unearthly-looking green wings, flew out of the shadows. It circled twice around Sad-face's head. Then it began a slow hovering dance in front of the cave.

Sad-face stared at it in horror. "Glory save us!" he muttered. Whirling, he dashed into the cave. The boys heard his voice continue in muffled tones: "We gotta get out of this crazy woods fast! I seen a moon-bird dancin' its evil spell. . . . We shouldn't have ever——"

"Rocks in your head," growled the other man. "Moon-birds yet!"

"Just the same, we're gettin' out of here," Sad-face insisted. "Those kids are on to us."

"I still ain't so sure."

"I told you," Sad-face argued, "that I spotted 'em with my field glasses when you were comin' in to the island this afternoon. They were trailin' you, all right, up on the road. They were made up like farmers, thinkin' we'd be dumb enough not to know who they were."

The other man grunted. "If I had my way we'd grab 'em and bring 'em here where they couldn't blab to the cops."

"Shut up, you two! We're leavin' like I said." This was a third man's voice, and Marvin thought it was time to get busy.

These men were crooks, all right. The plan of the raiding party must be carried out. He motioned to Eddie and they retreated over the rocks and down the path as swiftly as they could. The other explorers were waiting on the beach.

Marvin briefly told about the hideout, and he learned from the others that the *Spider Queen* and the motorboat lay hidden under some bushes a short distance down the other shore. Heywood reported that a well-worn path went inland from the anchorage. It should be simple to carry out the plan.

"Do you think we'll have time?" Bill asked, his eyes large in his round face. "The searching party coming and the crooks leaving——"

"We'll have to hurry." Marvin suddenly noticed the

headlights of several cars winking through the trees far down River Road. "The ice!" he whispered. "It's melted a little, so tighten the ropes on the four chunks we're carrying. Get the ropes off the others. Make it quick!"

Everyone leaped to the task, and in less than a minute they started around the island. Marvin, following Heywood and his handkerchief-covered flashlight, glanced up the river. There was a bobbing light on it now. They'd really have to hurry.

He patted the bulge in his uniform pocket. He wouldn't use the spider except as a last resort. He would sure hate to lose it—the biggest one, probably, in the whole county. And the meanest-looking, besides.

"Here's the barge, General," whispered Heywood, throwing his light beam on its blue rails for an instant. "And there's the path leading up. You go ahead and look for a place."

"Right."

"And make it quick," put in Emery. "This ice has got my britches wet."

The stealthy band went upward into the darkness of the woods. Shortly Marvin stopped. He pointed to a place where a large flat rock lay across the path, making a step about a foot and a half high.

"Just right," he said under his breath. "It'll save us

digging around. Fit the ice tight against the rock. Get the tops of the chunks level, and don't forget to take off the ropes. Miller Shaler, you're in charge of the ambush here. Corp Bluegate and I will proceed to reconnoiter."

"That's *corporal,* not corp," said Eddie. "I told you before."

"It'll be corpse," warned Bill, "if you don't pipe down. . . . I wonder if they have guns," he added in a hushed voice.

Tom shoved a block of ice in place. "Sure they have," he said. "You scared?"

"N-not me."

"They'll probably have their hands too full of swag to use them," Marvin guessed. "And remember, we have bigger guns than they have. In the dark they'll think they're real."

Emery impatiently swung a rope in his hand. "Aw, hurry up!" he said to Marvin. "And cut out the talking . . . sir."

Marvin and Eddie turned up the path, eyes and ears alert and guns ready. They had gone only a few steps when they heard low voices and saw a swinging light coming toward them. Quickly they slid into the foliage beside the path. By the lantern's light they could now see that there were two men—Flat-nose and Sad-face—and they were coming fast.

"That boat headin' down from Shalerville ain't a

healthy sign," said Sad-face, puffing. "And the cars on the road ain't goin' to no picnic."

As they passed Marvin and Eddie, Flat-nose glanced back. "What's keepin' the boss?" he grumbled.

"Leavin' a note for the milkman," replied Sad-face sarcastically.

Flat-nose suddenly yelped and shot off into space. The lantern he was carrying arched spectacularly through the trees and landed with a small explosion far down the path.

Sad-face stopped. He started to say something but only gurgled. Four shadowy forms had leaped from the woods and landed in a rolling heap on his friend. They were up again in no time, but Flat-nose lay sprawled on the ground. Sad-face stood for a moment as though staked to the ground. Then with a great effort he dashed forward.

"Hold 'em, Joe!" he called. "I'm coming!"

A second later Sad-face streaked across the ice and thudded onto Flat-nose's stomach. Ropes were whipped about his legs and arms, knots were tied, then all was quiet.

Heywood came up a moment later. "Didn't you say there were three?" he asked Marvin.

"Yeah. There's another."

"Maybe," said Eddie, "he heard the commotion and high-tailed into the woods."

A flashlight beam suddenly showed from a bend of the path above.

"Here he comes!" whispered Eddie. "I hope the fellows are ready with the ropes."

The third man approached rapidly and then passed them.

At that moment Sad-face called from below, "Scram back, Willie! The woods is full of white-faced pixies!"

A Continental sat on his mouth. But the warning had been heard and Willie turned to run. He took only one step before three peculiar characters blocked his retreat with flintlock muskets. Wide-eyed, he staggered back.

"Be-jabbers!" he muttered. "It's the pixie army with . . . with ten-foot cannons!" His flashlight clattered on the ground and rolled down the hill. Slowly he raised his trembling hands. "Wh-where you gonna take me?"

Heywood thoughtfully stroked his beard. "I think," he said in a hollow voice, "that you need a lesson in history."

"Huh?"

"My friends are not pixies. They are soldiers of the Continental Army. They have returned to haunt their bloody battlefield. The one on my left is George Washington himself, and he would be pleased to receive your salute."

The man stared.

"Salute, I said!" Heywood wiggled his gun.

Willie saluted.

"Now, turn around."

Willie turned.

"March!" Heywood ordered, prodding him with the musket. "March on to the icy floes of Valley Forge!"

Willie marched down the trail and hit the ice. He did a somersault as fancy as any the boys had ever seen. Rapidly gathering speed, he thumped and bounced downward along the path like a big rubber ball.

In a flash the Continentals were after him.

As Marvin hastily detoured around the ice he was alarmed to see their quarry straighten up and dash toward the shore.

"Rear guard!" Marvin shouted. "Don't let him get to the boats!"

Two giant firecrackers exploded. At the same moment Gilbert's rifle darted from the bushes. It caught the gang leader between his knees, and he thudded to the ground again.

"I'm shot!" he croaked, rolling back and forth in agony.

He suddenly found himself smothered with Continentals. Snarling like a baited tiger, he flung his assailants right and left. Then he lurched to his feet and once more started for the boat.

Marvin made a flying tackle. Willie twisted, then crumpled earthward.

Sitting solidly on the man's stomach, Marvin held a

mayonnaise jar close to his face. "If you don't hold still, mister," he warned, "you'll get this spider down your neck. It's a deathly black tarantula. It likes to bite, and it hasn't eaten for ten days."

As Marvin began to unscrew the jar lid the beam of a flashlight fell on the huge crouching spider. Willie's eyes bugged out. His Adam's apple bobbed up and down, but his voice had deserted him. Before he knew what was happening, his feet and arms were tightly bound with clothesline.

Marvin got up and looked at the gang leader's twitching face. There was something familiar about it—the long nose, the bald place on his head and the ear with the lobe cut off. Cut off in a fight?

Eddie, too, seemed to recognize the man. He started to say something to Marvin but was interrupted by the appearance of another light on the path above.

"Golly," whispered Bill, "we're all out of rope. We'll have to club this one with our——"

Marvin recognized the man behind the light. "Mr. Ziggley!" he shouted. "Watch out for the ice!"

But the mayor was already sailing through the air. He landed heavily on Flat-nose, who was just reviving from his earlier collision with Sad-face. *"Foof!"* went Flat-nose. *"Giant* pixies now!" he cried.

Mr. Ziggley got up. "Fool kids! Irresponsible, ungrateful bumpkins, running off in the boat and setting ding-busted traps!" He looked up at another light that was coming. "Watch it, Shaler!" he called. "These ingrates have greased the trail!"

Mr. Shaler saw the ice. He went around it and came down. For a long time he stood frowning at the three

silent men bound in clothesline. His gaze finally shifted to the rumpled Continentals, and he cleared his throat.

"Looks as if the mayor and I just missed the Battle of Trenton," he said. "We are now prepared to hear your report. Washington, what happened to this trio of Hessians?"

Marvin quickly whispered something to Eddie, then he faced Mr. Shaler. "Those two by the ice are Sad-face and Flat-nose," he said. "And this one is Wismer Woolsey."

Mr. Shaler's eyebrows rose. "Wismer Woolsey?"

"Yes. He's wanted by the Post Office Department for mail robbery. His picture's on the bulletin board. He lives in Camden. His alias is Willie Woodley, and his ear lobe got cut off in a fight."

"Hmm," said Mr. Shaler. He leaned over to look at the scowling criminal's ear.

"He's the gang leader," explained Eddie. "And those other men are his gang."

"I see." Mr. Shaler bent down and felt under Wismer's coat. When he stood up he held a revolver in his hand. "I see," he repeated seriously.

Turning to Emery, he said, "Take your flashlight and run across the island to where your boat is pulled up. Blink the light shoreward five times. There are a good many folks waiting."

Emery left and Mr. Shaler turned back to the boys. "Those folks' feelings are running pretty high. But I sincerely hope—" he grinned—"that your parents will be so relieved to find you alive that they'll forego giving you any painful lessons about the proper way to end a pageant."

Chapter 12

Cruise of the *Spider Queen*

OLD CAPPY got up from the running board of his truck and squinted at the seven boys who had gathered around him.

"Two black eyes," he counted, "one swoll lip, one scratched elbow and five bandages on as many differ'nt places." He thoughtfully rubbed his beard and added, "I hope your sittin' ends came through this commotion all right."

"Sure," said Marvin. His "sittin' end" was unharmed. But he would long remember the short, though forceful, lecture delivered by his father the night before.

Until his father had pointed them out, he had been unmindful of the real dangers involved in the expedition to the island. Now shivers ran up his back when he thought of the things that might have gone wrong.

Suppose the "borrowed" boat had struck a submerged rock off the beach? What if they had not found a place for the ice on the trail? Suppose the three criminals had not left the cave? Would they actually have mistaken the boys' guns for real ones and meekly followed orders? And suppose any of his friends had been badly injured or even shot? He, Marvin Tucker, would have been to blame. He felt overwhelmingly thankful that all had gone well.

"They brung in the barge this mornin'," Cappy said. He motioned toward the boatyard's inlet. "The motorboat, too. They was all gassed up an' ready to go somewhere."

Eddie nodded. "Mr. Shaler said they were going down to another hideout in Delaware Bay."

"Did the constabule find out for sure who they were?"

"It was Wismer Woolsey, all right," answered Gilbert. "And the other two were just ordinary crooks. They admitted the mail-truck robbery."

"And the super market and the big jewelry-store holdups, too," put in Emery. "But nobody's been able to find the loot. The robbers won't tell where it is, even if they go to jail for a hundred years apiece. . . . We're going to get a thousand dollars reward," he added as calmly as he could.

Cappy pulled out his pipe and began filling it from an oilskin pouch. "Reckon it's well deserved." He chuckled. "I sure would have give plenty t' have seen them fellers hit the ice blocks. But poor Mr. Ziggley—you shouldn't have done it to him. He's a fine, dignified mayor. I hear you crowned him oncet afore with butterfly nets. Must say I'm a mite surprised."

"Gee, we couldn't——" Marvin began, but he saw the twinkle in the old captain's eyes and knew that Old Cappy was teasing him. "What about the barge, Cappy?" he asked. "Is there any chance . . . Is that why Mr. Shaler told us to come here this morning?"

"Yep, that's why. He and I both figured maybe you should have first chance t' buy it."

Marvin swallowed hard. "Is . . . is it for sale? I sort of thought . . ."

"You thought it still belonged to Wismer and his handsome friends? Ord'narily it would, whether they'd be in jail or out, an' nobody'd be able to take it." Cappy paused to thump the truck's fender. "But this-here rattle-heap they traded t' me fer the barge was stolen."

"Stolen?" Seven mouths fell open.

"Yep. Stolen from a place over in Jersey just afore they showed up with it here. So the truck goes home, an' things is back t' where they was—with the barge tied up in the inlet, waitin' for a customer t' come and take a shine to her."

"Hot ziggedy!" cried Heywood. "Go get our Marvin, money . . . er, money, Marvin. She's gassed up to go!"

"Yeah!" Marvin ran for the road, but Cappy called him back.

"No need t' rush off for that. Mebbe, as long as you're all here, you'd like to take 'er out for a trial run. Ye know about outboard motors and navigatin', I reckon."

"Sure!" sang out seven voices.

"I understand ye done a good job last night, hittin' that little beach in the dark."

None of the boys heard Cappy's remark, for they were leaping over canoes, rowboats and smelly six-seaters on their way to the barge. One by one they thudded onto its deck.

Excitedly they ran up and down the length of the boat and into its cabin, getting the feel of its size and gauging its seaworthiness. At last, after waiting so long, they were on a boat of their own!

Marvin came over and stood beside Heywood, who was studying the motor. "How's it look to you?" he asked.

"She's a *beaut!*" Heywood grinned. "Sixteen horse-power and she'll make up to five thousand revs per minute. Maybe go twenty miles an hour at full power.... What do you say we give her that trial run?"

"Okay.... But wait. We have to christen her first."

"That's right. You got a bottle of something to bust on her?"

Old Cappy, who had been standing on the shore, gestured toward the supply shed. "One bottle comin' up," he said.

He went across the yard and soon returned with a bottle of lemon pop. He wrapped a strip of blue cloth around it like a ribbon, then ceremoniously handed it to Marvin.

"Thank you, Captain," said Marvin.

"Ye got a name for t' name 'er?"

"Yes. We had it when we came to buy the boat before. And we've planned the christening, too." Marvin turned. "All ashore!" he called. "Line up for the christening!"

The boys scrambled ashore and lined up along the bank.

"Ten-*shun!*" Marvin commanded.

The boys stiffened.

Old Cappy blinked his pale eyes. Then he removed his cap and shuffled to the end of the line, where he stood as straight as his bones would let him.

"Christener forward!" barked Marvin.

Emery, with the ribboned bottle of pop, took one pace ahead.

"Christener in position!"

Emery lay on his stomach at the edge of the bank and raised the bottle over the barge's bow.

Marvin glanced down the line. All eyes were fixed on the horizon. Not a muscle moved.

"O mighty barge, O master of mysterious shores," he intoned with ringing voice, "we now and forever christen thee *Spider Queen!*"

Emery swung at the bow. Pop spattered and broken glass plunked into the water of the inlet.

"At ease!" Marvin called, and the boys dashed again for the boat.

Old Cappy put on his cap. "That was a mighty movin'

cer'mony. Well, good fortune t' ye! She's a solid craft, an' if ye treat 'er good she'll take ye to them mysterious shores."

"Thanks." Marvin grinned. "We're going to take good care of her, all right." He stood in the stern while some of the others began untying the hawser. Something about the deck puzzled him—it didn't seem the same as when he had first seen the barge. He called Old Cappy over.

"Cappy, wasn't this deck made of wide boards running lengthwise, before?" he asked.

"Yep."

"Well, now they're narrow boards running across."

"Let's take a look." Cappy got into the boat and examined the deck. "Sure enough! Them burglars must've laid on a new one. For why, I don't know. The old one was bran' new."

Marvin suddenly remembered the stack of oak floorboards he and Eddie had seen in the pickup truck when they were loading it with groceries. Here were the same boards, laid over the old deck. But why? And where was all that tinned stuff? It hadn't been in the hideout. The cave had been just a small room with a table, some rickety chairs and three old mattresses in it. There had been no place to hide all those supplies.

"Say, Cappy," he said, "do you have a crowbar? I think there's something under these boards."

Cappy nodded and went again to his supply shed.

"You going to rip up our boat?" questioned Tom. "Before we even get started?"

"Just a couple of boards, to see if the gang stashed their food under the deck. They were planning a get-away, and with a boatload of supplies they could have stayed hidden for a year."

In a minute Cappy was back, and it took but another minute for the boys to pry up two of the oak boards. Bill, on hands and knees, peered underneath. Then he slowly sat up. "Do criminals just eat ketchup?" he asked.

The others got down to look. There was ketchup as far as they could see. But among the closely packed bottles was a large tin box which appeared too important to contain groceries. Heywood and Eddie quickly pried up another board and got the box out. When it was opened everyone gasped. It was packed to the brim with five, ten and twenty-dollar bills!

"Money!" shouted Emery, putting his nose in it. "The treasure of the Wismer Woolsey gang! We're rich! We're rich!"

Marvin frowned at him. *"Stolen* treasure," he said quietly. "It belongs to the super market."

"We'll have to turn it over to the constable," cautioned Gilbert.

Tom grabbed the crowbar. "Let's rip up the whole thing," he urged. "There's probably a million dollars under there and enough jewels to ransom a carload of kings!"

"Hey, wait!" Marvin put a hand on the crowbar.

Tom looked up. "Don't you want to find the loot?"

"Sure, but if we tear up the deck we'll have to unload all the canned food and the ketchup, as well as the loot. Then we'll have to stack it up and go to town for the constable and stand around waiting all day. Wouldn't you rather take a cruise first and do all that other stuff when we get back?"

Tom and the others definitely agreed. And in a few minutes Captain Marvin and his crew of six *putt-putted* out of the inlet. Heywood, the engineer, put the throttle on full speed and the *Spider Queen* proudly pushed its way upstream.

The voyagers were filled with a new and wonderful feeling. The thrill of it caught in their throats and shone in their eyes as they silently watched the rippling current of the Delaware slip past the sides of the boat. They were on an azure boat that promised rich adventure on distant and mysterious shores. The *Spider Queen* itself was a distant shore—a floating island in a boundless sea, known only to the seven.

The captain of this island sat on the cabin roof. With dreamy contentment he watched the dancing flashes of sunlight on the water of the surrounding sea. Suddenly he realized the sea had a bridge over it. It was the bridge to Bakerstown, and the *Spider Queen* was headed straight for one of its great stone piers!

"Ahoy!" was the first word he could get out. Then: "Hard to port! Bridge ahead!"

Heywood, snatched from his thoughts, pulled hard on the tiller, and the barge cleared the stone column by inches.

"Aye, aye, sir," he reported with relief.

"We need a system," Bill said. "We ought to have a watch in the crow's-nest."

Tom pushed back his sailor hat and gave Bill a disgusted look. "Motorboats don't have crow's-nests, ya goof."

"Then a watch *somewhere,*" argued Bill. "We can't go around bumping into bridges and things."

"And we need another mate at the tiller," put in Emery, "in case the driver gets sick."

Marvin half lowered his eyelids at Emery. "On a vessel, we don't call the steerer a driver. He is known as the helmsman."

"Yeah," added Bill. "He watches the binnacle."

"We got a binnacle?" asked Heywood.

"Who knows? We haven't had this boat very long."

"If it ever had any binnacles," said Tom, "Old Cappy would have scraped them off."

"You're thinking of barnacles, stupid!" Eddie was eying the deck with interest. Finally he could stand it no longer; he picked up the crowbar and pried off another board.

Marvin heard the squeak of the nails and turned around. "If you pull up the deck," he warned, "you'll have to walk on ketchup and beans."

"I just thought I'd take off a couple more boards."

"We could take them *all* up," suggested Emery, "and put them back as we go along."

Gilbert peered wisely over the rims of his glasses. "We wouldn't have to nail them down again."

"Okay," assented Marvin. "But I have to stay up here to watch where we're going, and Heywood has to steer."

The good ship *Spider Queen* moved placidly up the river, accompanied by the screech of protesting nails. One by one the deckboards came up. Dozens of cans which had once loaded Mr. Pratt's shelves were revealed. Halfway down the deck the searchers discovered another box. It held the "king's ransom" in jewels—from the Trenton jewelry store, according to the labels. A third box, discovered near the cabin, contained several registered letters from the mail robbery, and many tied-up bundles of paper money.

There were no more boxes. When the last board had been put back, the boys stowed the treasure in the cabin and then scattered over the barge to enjoy the remainder of the voyage.

"One thousand dollars," mused Heywood with a sigh that was heard the length of the boat. "Boy, what we could do with that!"

"There's a lot more than a thousand," scoffed Tom. "Those jewels alone——"

"I was thinking about the reward we're going to get for capturing Wismer Woolsey," said Heywood. "What'll we do with it?"

Marvin gazed at the near-by shore line. "Emery and I have to put our shares in the bank, Dad says."

"We'll get bankbooks," explained Emery. "And then take the money out again."

Bill grunted. "Sounds nuts to me."

"No bankbooks for me," put in Eddie. "I'm going to spend mine for some camping stuff. We'll need it if we go up to Locust Island. How about going tomorrow? We could stay a week and live in the robbers' cave."

"Why just a week?" Bill asked. "With a barge full of grub we could stay until the cave got too full of snow to sit down."

Marvin, on the cabin roof, suddenly grabbed at something that flew past his face. He peered intently shoreward for a moment, then called out, "Hard to port!"

Obediently Heywood swung the tiller. "When are you going to learn a new command?" he grumbled.

"Easy into shore," Marvin ordered. "Take her slow to that tree that's fallen over the water."

"Aye, sir! But why? Boats don't land in trees."

"Quarter speed, now."

"Aye, sir!"

The barge slowed to a crawl and inched closer to the branches of the tree. Marvin got to his feet and took his cap off. "Brake, full stop!"

The cabin brushed against the leaves. Marvin leaned far over and swung his cap. "Got him!" he shouted. "Boy, is he a whopper!"

"Who's a whopper?" asked Emery.

"Reverse engine!"

"You gone nuts?"

Marvin gave his number-two scowl to Emery, then called again to the helmsman: "Full speed astern!"

"Aye, sir," muttered Heywood. The *Spider Queen* backed away from the tree, churning water as she gathered speed.

"What have you got in your cap?" blurted Emery.

Marvin grinned. "It's a praying mantis, nosey. The biggest, greenest——"

"Hey, Captain!" called Heywood. "You want this barge to back into New Jersey?"

"Whoa!" cried Marvin. "I mean, turn downriver to the Kinnecong dock—the home port of the *Spider Queen*. Full speed ahead!"